Dakhmeh

Naveed Noori

Dakhmeh

The Toby Press

First English Language Edition 2003

The Toby Press LLC
www.tobypress.com

ISBN 1 902881 77 X *paperback*

A CIP catalogue record for this title
is available from the British Library

Typeset in Garamond by Jerusalem Typesetting

Printed and bound in the United States by
Thomson-Shore Inc., Michigan

A glossary of the Persian terms used in this book may be found at the end

Day 1

Evin is not such a bad place so long as you are left alone. These are mild times, I think they have almost forgotten how to torture. And for a price you can buy anything, even freedom. But if you should find yourself without money, then even obtaining a pen can be a very difficult matter.

Yes, where to begin? Should I go back 2500 years, or 1250, 200, or 20? It is all the same road that has led me to this particular place. Revolution, what a romantic word! One almost imagines a fiery youth standing victorious atop a hill, brandishing a flag in one hand and a rifle in the other, a symbol of the triumph of weak over strong, right over wrong. But don't let them fool you. Revolution can be a terrible thing, a horrible thing. One cursory look at the French Revolution would tell such a story. And yet, at times, it is as inevitable as an earthquake, when the forces pitted against each other for centuries past suddenly give way, like tectonic plates that slide past one another, reducing everything around them to rubble.

How is one to give meaning to events so momentous? There are those who study revolutions all their lives, who sift through the rubble to decipher some kind of pattern, much like the seismologist who tries to predict the next earthquake. And then there are those whose lives are the rubble, who stand dazed in the aftermath and are never quite the same. The least you can do, anyone can do, is to look at the facts, and to do so we would have to go back to where it all started.

This is an arduous task, no doubt, but I have had months to ruminate on those events. The first task at hand is to go to the point where I entered this play. As I lie here during the day, look-

ing straight up these high walls that enclose me, I can still see a bit of sky, just over the topmost part of the window, between the bars. A sliver is all I get, but even for this I am grateful.

The sky can become so blue with just a tinge of paleness, and still, without a cloud, without interruption, an overarching roof that is both comforting and endless in its power. I imagine it was this same sky that inspired the lovely blue-tiled mosques of Isfahan, and it was this same sky that was present in the plains and desert around Takht-e Jamshid and Pasargrade, even Karbala. We left it behind, those who went west to Europe and America; or earlier, those who fled east to India and China.

Gazing up at this blue are some of my first memories. Those early memories are patchy and without sound, a silent colorful movie. The later ones I remember in much more detail. Through the years, how often I would play them back, scene by scene; slowly retracing all those steps I refused to let go. I was the keeper of the holy fire, responsible for stoking each and every memory. I did a good job of it, too, for years anyway. How ironic that it was the very act of preservation that led to the decay. But day by day I am reclaiming them, or they me, as they seep back into my being. Once they take hold, I can scarcely think of anything else until the cycle exhausts itself. But now I can write, and this will help ease my mind.

My first trip to the bazaar, what a sight! My sister Naazi, my mother, and I had gone there together. I held on tightly to Naazi's hand, and she to our mother's. All I could see were legs going in every direction, jostling and bumping against me, completely oblivious of my small and frail body. I was terrified and stayed close to Naazi who seemed not to be bothered by the commotion. Every now and then she would pull me out of the way of a speedy moped or a careless coolie. I didn't even have a chance to see any of the stores. Then, ahead of us a clearing opened and, to my amazement, we were standing in front of the toy stand.

Though my head barely reached the counter, I took it all in. Until then toys were given as gifts, suddenly appearing in the hands of someone entering through the door of our home. Now I stood at the place where all the toys came from. The toys were of every imaginable shape and color, hanging on both sides of the kiosk, which seemed to stretch forever.

The owner, smiling, wound up a mechanical ladybug that was painted red and black and let it loose on the counter. I was mesmerized by the spinning movement and the crunching sounds of the gears. But it was too late. I had already spotted the cork guns. I pointed to one and he handed it to me. I took aim at Naazi and pulled the trigger, letting the cork fly. It did not actually hit her as the cork was jerked back in mid-flight by the string attached to it. Naazi was so excited that she wanted one also. My mother tried to distract us with the laughing box, a small plastic box with a button that, when pressed, let loose a roomful of laughter. That held our attention for about thirty seconds before we went back to the cork guns. My mother tried to show us the other toys but it was the cork guns that we walked away with.

That afternoon we searched the skies for crows to shoot down. Their bodies gray and wings black, they would fly above us, going from perch to perch as soon as we took aim.

We were in the enclosed courtyard of a decrepit building that belonged to my father's aunt. She was the figure in the distance, on the other side of the *hoez*, wearing a *chador*, which covered her from head to foot so thoroughly that I no longer remember her face.

She was affectionate but I think we were too young to understand. We didn't know her that well and so shied away from her. My only clear memory of her is from that moment, standing on the other side of the yard, her back slightly bent.

At night we slept on the floor of an old room. The wooden shutters were kept open to let in fresh air. Lying on our mats, we could see the night sky and the moon above the courtyard. Our pillows were large and cylindrical, with the guns safely tucked underneath them. When I woke up in the morning, the first thing I did was reach under the pillow for my gun. I felt nothing, so I *lifted up the pillow and checked the mat on which I was sleeping. The gun was missing. I woke up Naazi and, to her dismay, we discovered that her gun was also gone.*

We were told a thief had come in the middle of the night and stolen our guns. It seemed like a plausible story, because that very night I had gone to bed with gallant dreams of foiling robberies with my newly acquired weapon. We were terribly upset at first, but we soon found the pleasures of chasing tiny earthen-colored lizards in the courtyard, hoping to break off their tails and watch as they wiggled for minutes afterwards. Usually, the lizards were too fast for us, allowing us to get within a certain predetermined distance before scurrying into the cracks in the wall.

There was an old cook there who had a limp and walked with a cane. He came over and told us not to fall asleep in the courtyard. He knew a man who had done just that and had woken up hearing noises and feeling strange sensations in his ear. A lizard had crawled into his ear. And when he had tried to pull it out, the tail detached, scaring the lizard, making it go further into the man's ear and brain. We were terrified that night, and only went to sleep after stuffing our ears with cotton-balls.

Many years later my mother confessed to confiscating the guns, fearing that the projectile cork would damage our eyes. My father had already passed away, and I think this made our mother overly protective of us.

The sky has remained with me as has the image of a bent old lady with a chador. *What all this has to do with anything, I don't know, except being the first of a continuous line of events that make up my life, as I remember it.*

My childhood itself was relatively uneventful. I suppose the death of my father was a big event, but I don't remember it. Growing up, I did not know what I was missing. At school, when the children spoke of their fathers I would remain silent. Otherwise, the only noticeable difference was that the rest of our relatives, out of pity, would shower us with more attention and gifts.

We went to a private school early on, learning both Persian and French, the latter of which I would forget over the years. Those days of elementary school were happy times. I do not think about them much, and right now I can't remember anything out of the ordinary—maybe that is what a childhood should be like, but I am getting off track here…

The pen-and-paper problem had started innocently enough—with just a hello. But Nabi *Khan's** greeting had quickly turned into a dilemma. In all his years working at Evin he had never been in such a position, caught between a prisoner and the administration. He was the custodian, lowest in the prison hierarchy, but a member nonetheless.

Nabi Khan had said hello back. Maybe this was the way of the older generation, but that was how it was, the reply to a greeting was always met courteously, regardless of the other's station in life. The prisoner had then engaged him in small talk, which made him feel even more uneasy.

Throughout the years, he had come to know many of the prisoners, but that was an entirely different matter. He could not help coming into contact with them. It was his job to take food to the prisoners, even those in isolation. He would also have to sweep the halls and do other sundry tasks depending on the situation. In this way he came to know many of the prisoners by sight and name. But if they asked Nabi Khan any personal questions he would usually reply, "Don't ask questions."

He only rarely saw the ones in isolation. If he happened to be in the hallway when one was being brought in or transferred, he would stop what he was doing and move to the side as the procession of guards and shackled prisoner went by. Though he had never seen this one, he could tell the crime by the youthful sound of his voice and refined content of his speech. These prisoners were members of the middle class, nearly always young and invariably political.

He felt sorry for him, that's probably where all the trouble started. The prisoner's everyday meal was that of bread and water. This meager meal was even worse than what the violent criminals were given. But Nabi Khan had no control over this. These decisions were made in one of the offices he cleaned in the evening. Furthermore, the trays were filled by someone else; he was only the distributor.

* *Khan,* see Glossary. Though used henceforth as Nabi's surname, *Khan* is neither a surname nor a 'ruler,' as in the English definition. It is used as a quasi-title, like 'Sir,' among members of the lower class.

There were other reasons why he pitied him. The prisoner was one of the forgotten ones—he had been there for months already. Those in isolation were usually transients; they were there for a short disciplinary period before being transferred to the regular ward or even released. The occasional few who stayed longer usually came to a bad end. Where was his family? he wondered. It was strange that there had been no mail for him, but maybe it was being withheld. Nabi Khan did not even know his name until one day the prisoner had introduced himself as Arash.

Nabi Khan was Arash's only link to the outside world. Nabi Khan was aware of this and could not help but feel a certain satisfaction when talking to him. Not that they ever got beyond *taroaf* and the weather in the few moments before he delivered or collected his tray. To do so would be an open invitation to danger. Once people started talking, there was no telling how the matter would end. And when, one day, Arash had asked for a pen and paper, Nabi Khan did not reply. He left hastily, as if he had not heard him. After all, there was an iron door between them and he very well may not have heard him.

Nabi Khan gave a lot of thought to Arash's request. This was not the first time a prisoner had wanted something. Usually, they even offered money, but it had always been for something he could not provide, be it a better meal or freedom. The rest of the things they bought from each other or the guards. But this was an easy matter. What was a pen and a few pieces of paper?

He tried to examine all the issues surrounding this matter, taking into account the small but potential risk involved. He even considered whether Arash's friendliness was for the sole purpose of using him. Thus, Nabi Khan was altogether cautious and waited a long time before making a decision. He instinctively knew that he should not help the prisoner, but in the ensuing weeks his mind gradually changed. He was finally won over when he saw that Arash never brought up the matter again.

Nabi Khan came to work each day by bicycle. It took him almost two hours to get there in the morning. It was a strenuous ride, nearly uphill all the way, except for the last stretch which was downhill and steep. For part of the way he had to take the Moddaress Expressway and deal with the multitude of cars swerving in and out of the fluid lanes. He could not think about getting hit, it was God's will, anything He desires, he thought. In the morning, though, more often than not, there were traffic jams for kilometers on end, and he would easily pedal past the stranded cars. If he was running late and there was no traffic, he would have to flag down a taxi and place his bike in the trunk of the Paykan. The other passengers were usually annoyed at the extra time he required to secure his bike, but the driver did not mind receiving double the fare for a few moments pause. Nabi Khan was never that late to begin with and usually going to the next big roundabout was all that was needed.

The ride back, by contrast, was easy. He would walk his bike out of the guarded prison entrance. The gates would then close behind him and he would continue walking up the hill. Once at the top, the rest of the ride home required very little pedaling. It was then that he had a chance to look around.

Tehran at dusk, he would sometimes think, what could be prettier? The asphalt gave back to the city all the heat it had gathered during the day, and the city gave back to the people all of the day's pent-up fumes.

As he drove by the cars stuck in traffic, he would smile. The morning's hard work was being repaid to him now. When the traffic was not slowed to a halt, it moved in torrents, the cars honking and zigzagging around each other. He did not like getting caught behind the buses which spewed continuous streams of black clouds into the air.

Once off the main streets, the pace was less frenzied and he could see the people close up, one step nearer to their homes, as was he. By now it was evening. There were only a few people left on the streets. The schoolchildren were already home and had changed out of their uniforms. The boys were usually playing football on his street. The sounds of their shouts and the plastic ball skipping along the asphalt wound through the alleys and met him a few blocks from home. He would hear their mothers yell, "Hossein, come inside for dinner," or, "Mammad, the food is getting cold!"

As the sounds of their game receded into the distance, the call to prayer broadcasted over the loudspeakers echoed through the streets. The mosque was not close to his house, so he could also hear the call of another muezzin, like an echo, during the pauses and silences of the first. After reaching his house, he would wash the dust and grime from his hands and face, drops of black water falling off his skin. When the days were short, he would pray before he ate his dinner. This was his favorite time, when the worries and hustle of the day disappeared with the setting sun, and he would have time to spend with his wife.

One day after work he stopped by his neighborhood grocery store. I haven't bought a notebook since my grade school days, he thought, smiling to himself. That's not it, he thought again, it was when my sons were in school, over 30 years ago.

That night, he told his wife. He had thought she might object because the man he was helping was a prisoner or that they had to spend their own money. But paper was cheap, and he had not spent any more than he occasionally gave to beggars. His wife did not seem interested one way or another.

The next day, before Nabi Khan went to deliver the prisoner's meal, he placed the notebook under the bread and the pen next to the bowl of water. He had not even considered giving it secretly because suspicion would have immediately fallen on him. Instead, he told the two guards in charge of isolation, "Listen, this prisoner has been bugging me about pen and paper for weeks now. I'm going to give it to him just to shut him up, is that alright?"

One guard shrugged his shoulder and said, "Sure, I don't care."

The other asked, "What do you think he wants it for anyway?"

Nabi Khan said, "I don't know, maybe to write his confessions."

Nabi Khan turned around and started to walk down the

hallway. The guards looked at each other silently, one raised his eyebrow. Nabi Khan, unaware of this exchange, continued walking with the tray.

The prisoner's cell was the at the end of the hallway. Before he slipped the tray through the slot, he paused for a second and was about to whisper, "Be careful."

The guards were all the way at the other end of the hall, too far to hear anything. But he held his tongue. He thought he had done enough already. And this was Evin, he should know by now, he needed no such warning.

England had not allowed him entry into their land, yet he was granted the title of Sir. I think he was the sort of person who would get into trouble regardless of the regime, be it the Shah, Khomeini, Mossadegh. Yes, to be young and a radical, antiestablishment. And now he had become infamous; no, not of his own doing—some even thought he was an English spy! But where would we be if we could not even blame the British for such a trifling matter?

If these accounts seem tame and my thoughts coherent, forgive me. I have had ample time on my hands and time enough to reflect. There will be those who come forward and say how such and such episode happened differently, and they very well may be right. At the time the events seemed to move so swiftly that I now feel I was just bouncing around, reacting without thought.

Even after all the deliberation over the past months while waiting for this pen, I feel I am diverging from the chronological path I sought to follow. The pen is taking its own course.

Sir Buckley's prison was not the Shah's or Khomeini's, but that of Western civilization. I remember arriving at Terminal 1, Charles de Gaulle Airport, Paris. It was my first time in France, and being between flights and waiting for the one to Tehran, I took a stroll around the terminal. I spent my time watching the people from around the world and occasionally venturing into a store to look at the various articles for sale.

When I tired of this, I sat down for a rest. On the lower

level, I chose a spot between the pizza shop and electronics store. I put my belongings at my feet and sat next to an ordinary-looking man. Almost immediately I went into my own thoughts so that I scarcely noticed him.

What would Tehran be like? I had read all the recent articles, I had seen the photos, but I still wondered. Would I fit in? I knew I had a bit of an accent from being away for all those years, and my clothes, too, would give me away. Perhaps the most important question was precisely what I was doing and why.

For years my thoughts had been with Iran. At night, I would lay in a trance, delving into memories, retracing each step, revisiting each corner as if it were new, until hours later, exhausted, the scattered images transformed into dreams.

But in the weeks before I left, I felt a numbness set in. I did not so much as give a thought to my upcoming trip. The practical preparations were done efficiently, that was all. How often I had longed for that moment when I would again set foot in my own country, my homeland, Iran. I kept Molaana's poem close to my heart all those years, believing that someday Joseph would return to Canaan. But now, as the momentous day neared, it was not joy but a listlessness that gripped me.

At Charles de Gaulle, the numbness started to fade, and in its place apprehension, joy, fear, and other contradictory feelings flooded in. It was at this point that he turned to me and said, "Salaam Agha*.*"

Not the least bit surprised, I spoke back in Persian.

"Salaam, how are you doing?"

"Very well, thank you. Are you looking forward to your trip to Iran?"

It was then that I took notice of him, and the first thing that struck me was his raspy, tobacco-laden voice. He was a skinny, balding, middle-aged Iranian man, wearing a thin, well-groomed

* *Agha*, see glossary. *Agha* is a title denoting deference, like Mr. or Sir.

mustache, with typical black eyebrows and brown, almond-shaped eyes. He had a small mouth and was sucking on a pipe as he smiled. A large luggage cart was next to him, containing various boxes and suitcases, all stacked neatly.

He nodded and looked at the ticket I was holding in my hand. "I saw your ticket," he said, blowing out a puff of smoke, "but tell me, why are you going?"

"I haven't been there for many years…"

He shrugged his shoulders and said, "I haven't been there for years either. But why go? Iran is unpredictable. There is no rhyme or reason. The whole country is like one large prison. And what will you do about the draft?"

I had heard all these arguments many times before and seeing how skeptical he was, I did not tell him I was coming here for good; rather, I gave the more moderate reply of, "The situation has changed in the last couple of years. By all accounts the regime is more moderate. This is the right time to go."

He took the pipe out of his mouth and started laughing heavily, slapping his hands on his knees. "They're going to eat you up alive, do you hear me?! You will never survive. Don't you know anything? Did you talk to anyone before buying your ticket? You are too much!"

Sir Buckley continued laughing. I was slightly taken aback, but resolute nonetheless that I knew what I was doing.

He said, "Tell me, are the Akhounds *still in power?"*

"What do you mean? Of course—"

"Then nothing has changed. If you place all the perfume in the world into a cesspool, it will still stink like the shit it is."

Then he became more serious, "Let me tell you a story, my story. Every day journalists come from all over the world to hear my story, but you are here already, and I haven't spoken Persian in a long time. So listen…

This airport is my home and prison. I came here in November 1988 with a one-way ticket to England. Somewhere en route from the train station to here, all my documents were stolen—I mean everything! My visas, passport, papers for political asylum. After much discussion, the French officials even allowed me to go to England. I actually made it there without the proper documents, but the English turned me away. Now I spend my days and nights here. I am in limbo. At first the French people were hostile towards me, but they have grown used to me, and I even have a few friends here in the airport. They bring me food and other day-to-day things. Over the years I have seen many things here, people from all over the world.

I once saw the French Police stop an Iranian couple, right here in front of us. They opened their suitcases on the ground and emptied everything on the floor—their clothes, gifts—everything. The couple stood silently, shocked and humiliated. The other passengers stared at them like they were criminals. The police found nothing and gave no explanation, no apology. And why should they when they do not consider us human? They treat us like the Algerians here. The police left the mess on the ground and moved on. I talked to the couple afterwards, the man was even an engineer, educated in the West. Imagine that! But don't get the wrong idea. I tell you all this as a comparison.

There is a doctor here, at the airport, by the name of Philippe Hulot. The way he speaks to the press! As if I were his personal lab rat he gets pleasure out of observing. He says that when I leave here, I will have to be weaned off the airport like a drug addict. What an idiot! Mardeh hesabi, *even if what he is saying is true, if he thinks I am his patient, what kind of doctor would talk to the press about his patients like that?*

I am the new Turk, the new "Sick Man of Europe." At times they like to remind us who is the master, the sahib. But don't get me wrong. No, I tell you all this as a comparison. These people are my jailers, but they leave me alone. Look at me. Would you think I was a prisoner by how I am dressed or how I am free to go about here?"

It was true, he was not a prisoner in the conventional sense. His clothes were impeccable, he was clean shaven, and within the confines of the terminal he was free to move about and do as he pleased.

"This is my prison," he continued, "but all in all it's not so bad compared to Iran. I've been in prison in Iran. Even daily life there is like being in prison. No, thank you, I'd rather stay here. Take a piece of advice from me—don't go."

I thought to myself what an incredible story. I asked, "But how is it, isn't there anyone who can help you?"

"I have a lawyer who has been working on my case for years; he says that I may be able to leave in a few months, but he always says that."

"And then where will you go?"

He became quiet.

"That's a problem—I don't know. I'm old now, almost fifty. I don't have a wife or children. What am I to do? My prime years were wasted on politics, and almost a decade in this place. It is so easy to say ten years, isn't it? But where have they gone, who will give them back to me? This is the only life I will ever live. I sometimes wonder if anyone really cares about the life of another or if it's just words on paper. I think those who are not in jail or dying have no conception of time, of how precious life is. Look around you, everyone is busy with the present, thinking this will last forever."

He was quiet again. Trying to gauge his true feelings on Iran, I asked him, "Would you ever consider going back to Iran?"

"Haven't you heard what I've been telling you? I would rather die than go back. My name is Sir Buckley here, not Sassan. I am sure they know about me, they read the articles. If I fly to Iran, what's to stop them from taking me off the airplane and accusing me of being a British spy? What defense could I give? The guilt lies in the name. Besides, there is a reason I left in the first place."

There was a long pause. It was then that the absurdity of

his name struck me and I asked him, "Why do they call you Sir Buckley?"

Sassan was staring at the ground, then he looked up at me and said, "Those French Immigration bastards. When I was turned back from England, they all seemed so happy in my failure. They all laughed when they saw me coming back, walking down that corridor. That is what my life had become, a joke. One of them said, 'Look! Sir Buckley's back!' They laughed even more."

During the telling of his life story, filled with its numerous travails and disappointments, never did he seem bitter, save at that particular moment. He shook his head, raised his hands in the air, palms up, and woefully said, "The name has stuck."

I spent the next several hours with Sassan and we talked more about his bureaucratic entanglement. Soon we decided it was best to continue our talk in the nearby bar.

The place was bustling with a continuing stream of passengers but we found two empty stools at the bar.

The bartender, a young French man, smiled when he saw Sassan and spoke to him in French, "Hello, haven't seen you in a while."

I knew enough French to understand that part, but there quickly followed a series of exchanges where I understood nothing.

The bartender then glanced over at me and asked Sassan, "Another Iranian boy you're sending home?"

"Jean, I have a duty to send them off the right way!" Sassan said in half-jest.

Sassan looked over to me and asked, "Do you speak any French?"

"I once knew a little."

"Do you speak English?" Sassan then asked me.

"Yes."

Sassan looked over to the bartender and asked, "And you don't speak any English?"

"Very little."

Sassan turned to me, using his right hand to give a gesture of introduction, "Arash." He then turned to Jean, gesturing with his left hand, "Jean."

Jean and I shook hands. In his broken English, Jean said, "I tell you with good—"

Turning to Sassan, Jean began to ask him something then he said, "Never mind! Arash he will drunk you! Iran—danger!"

"And why shouldn't we get drunk?" Sassan turned to me while shaking his head, "If you allow them to affect your actions outside of Iran, then you're in trouble."

For the next few hours we drank in earnest. Soon there was no turning back—Jean kept passing us the drinks, and we kept getting more drunk. Sassan and I were almost face-to-face, but now I forget half of what we talked about. I do remember smoking Sassan's pipe when I turned to him and said, "Sassan, I have a confession to make."

"Well, what is it?"

"I'm going to Iran to stay."

"OO-HOO, I thought you were going to tell me you're a relative of the Shah! So this isn't just some trip where you see your relatives here and visit there, and then get back on the plane and tell everyone how horrible the situation in Iran is. But let me tell you something—it is that bad, and you haven't even lived there all these years. You'll see how it's changed, it's not a place to live anymore."

"I know it won't be perfect, or close to what it was, but it will be something."

"Well, you're even crazier than I thought. Everyone gets homesick, but going to stay... You had better drink up."

He saw my hesitation and raised his glass, saying, "Drink up, I said!"

"Do you think I'll have enough time to sober up on the plane?" I asked him.

"Why would you want to do something like that? Being drunk is the perfect way to make your entrance. It will make

you numb. And trust me, you will have to be numb to all that is around you in order to survive."

"But what if they smell it on my breath?"

He looked at me for a moment and said, "Even though you're drunk, you have a point there. Maybe we should stop. The last thing I need now is your blood on my hands."

Sassan and I thanked Jean and staggered back to the bench. Periodically, people would bring him packages. He would thank them gratefully and place them by his side. Such was his character that he accepted these items as gifts or something to be repaid, and not as handouts.

When it was time to leave, he walked me to my gate. We said our goodbyes and kissed each other on the cheeks. He turned to the stewardess accepting the boarding cards and said, "Take care of my friend here."

Then another stewardess came up and greeted Sassan. He whispered something in her ear. She smiled and replied, "Of course."

Then Sassan turned to me, "Well my boy, I see your mind is set. There are many beautiful things that I miss, don't get me wrong, and I still do love Iran. Please do one thing for me…"

"Anything you want," I said, expecting him to ask me to deliver a message to a family member.

He looked at me with a mock severity and said, "Go and piss on Khomeini's grave for me!"

He burst out laughing, slapped his hands on his thighs, and started to walk back towards his bench.

Arash wrote a few more lines before he suddenly stopped writing. He tore out the pages and started chewing on them. Then he wrote the following:

Day 1

In the name of Allah, the Compassionate and Merciful.

Evin is not at all like I had imagined it. My room is spacious. It has a lovely skylight. They feed me adequately—I never go hungry. Every day they bring my medicine on a tray with a glass of water. Even my pen and paper, one of the attendants was kind enough to give it to me for free. Human rights are respected here, who says otherwise? Thanks to Allah, we have Islamic institutions with just rules and regulations, respect and dignity for the human being.

Where to begin and where to end?

Before coming to Tehran, I had a stopover in France. By accident, by pure coincidence, I sat next to one of my Moslem brethren. Praise Allah! His name was Hassan. He was middle-aged and balding, with prayer beads in his hand, saying a prayer. We soon began talking, of Islam, of Iran, of all the improvements since the Revolution, the importance of religion and a theocracy, the everyday happiness in society, women's newfound respect in society, the many financial and cultural advances. He asked me why I was going back to Iran. I told him to perform my Islamic duty by helping the country, to live Islamically and to spread the Revolution if called upon. In short, I had become West-toxicated and could no longer stand it.

His first name was Hassan, but I do not recall his family name or where he was traveling to. But we prayed together in the airport. Before I boarded the plane he turned to me and said, "Please do one thing for me when you go to Iran…"

"Anything you wish."

"Please go to Imam Khomeini's shrine and say a prayer for him from me."

"I promise that I will."

We kissed and parted. I eagerly awaited my flight to Tehran.

When I got to Mehrabad Airport, I changed $20 at the bank. I took a taxi to the Hotel Evin. I stayed there for a few days, mostly *in my room. I ordered* chelo kabob *from room service, watched TV, and read the newspapers. I didn't talk to anyone then. One of the hotel workers told a Turkish joke. I laughed.*

I almost forgot: I had a

Before Arash had finished writing that first page and eating the other pages, the door of his cell opened. The guards took one step back, making grimaces. One said, "What a bad smell!"

Arash busied himself with swallowing the paper that was still in his mouth. One of the guards picked up the few crumpled pages and tore out the lone written page in his notebook. The other one came up and blindfolded Arash. He was shackled and led out to the hall. Nabi Khan, who was sweeping the hallway, stood to one side and looked at Arash, not believing that this was the same person he had talked to.

Arash's hair was all matted and in knots. He had an unkempt beard. The expression on his face was detached, showing neither fear nor joy. His fingernails were long and filthy. Above all, he was terribly skinny, having more in common with a South Tehrani drug addict than any political prisoner he had ever seen. He could not reconcile the voice with the person in front of him.

Had Nabi Khan seen Arash before, he would not have even considered giving him the notebook, as now he felt more revulsion than pity. I was foolish, he later thought, I should have mailed the notebook anonymously—then he would have his notebook and I wouldn't have to worry—or to hell with his pen and paper, I shouldn't have gotten involved at all.

* * *

Nabi Khan was called to the office. He was asked a few questions and was promptly fired. He gathered his things and went to the courtyard where he kept his bicycle. Nabi Khan was dejected and deep in thought. Walking with his bicycle towards the gate, he motioned for the guard to open it. He walked through it and heard the gate close behind him.

He had done nothing wrong. Still, he thought, I am lucky to walk through that gate, to walk away from Evin. He now began to walk on the sidewalk, up the hill. What was he to do now? How was he to work and where? Again he thought it had been foolish to get involved, but it was just a pen and some paper. How dangerous was that to anyone? As he walked along the steepest part, he took a deep breath and sighed. His time at Evin was finished and a part of him started to rejoice. It was oppressive in there, it was a prison after all, not any prison, but Evin. Maybe this was God's will, *ghessmat*, His way to get him out of there.

In the midst of these thoughts a black Mercedes with tinted windows crept up beside him, slowing down to his pace. The engine was so quiet that Nabi Khan did not even notice it until the back window came down and a man asked, "Father, do you need a lift?"

Nabi Khan was at once startled and, when he saw the car, terrified. But he tried to stay calm. He recognized the man in the back from the prison. Nabi Khan said, "No, thank you very much, I am used to going this way."

The man in the Mercedes said, "Look, there is no need for *taroaf*, where do you live?"

By now both the car and Nabi Khan had stopped. Nabi Khan said, "Near Enghelaab roundabout, *Ghorbon*."

"Then you have to get in, I insist."

"But—"

"No," said the man loudly, raising his hand, "I won't hear it."

He then ordered the driver, "Put the bike in the trunk."

The driver got out of the car and walked toward Nabi Khan, whose hands firmly gripped the handle bars. The driver placed his hands on the bike and looked at Nabi Khan with annoyance. Nabi Khan let go as he knew he had no choice. Nabi Khan got into the back seat, leaving the door open. The driver placed the bike in the trunk, closed the door on Nabi Khan's side, and got behind the wheel. The car moved forward as Nabi Khan's window went up by itself and he heard the doors lock.

The seat covers were made of leather and freshly polished; there was a window between the front and back seats. The windows and locks were controlled by a panel of buttons next to the man beside him. At another time these things would have impressed him deeply and he would have been sure to remember every detail to tell his wife and his children. Now they only added to his unease.

Nabi Khan had seen this man from time to time. He had been in Evin that very day. When Nabi Khan was called into the office, the man was in the room next door, drinking a cup of tea and smiling at someone. He was always smartly dressed, wearing glasses and had a neatly trimmed beard. Everyone, it seemed, treated this man with the kind of respect no one else garnered—not even the warden. That was all Nabi Khan knew about him.

"My name is Mr. Soleymaani, pleased to meet you."

Nabi Khan wiped his sweaty palms on his trousers and shook the man's hand, "My name is Nabi Khan, pleased to meet you."

Oh God, what have I gotten myself into, he thought.

"Nabi Khan, you mean to tell me that you ride your bike from all the way there to Evin every day?"

"Yes, *Ghorbon*."

"Why not the bus?"

"The bus?" Nabi Khan replied.

"Yes."

"Because I have no money."

"Ah…" Mr. Soleymaani said, absently looking out the window, "no money."

Mr. Soleymaani became silent. After several minutes, he touched Nabi Khan on the shoulder and said, "I tell you what, the driver here will drop me off at home and then he will take you to your house."

Nabi Khan, who had almost jumped at his touch, said, "But *Ghorbon*, this is plenty so far."

"But we've made your way longer already, you told me you live near Enghelaab, right? No, no, he will drive you."

Nabi Khan was leaning forward, sitting on the edge of his seat thinking, oh God, please help me, please help this one time. He then became aware of his awkward position in the seat and sat back. Mr. Soleymaani lit a cigarette and offered him one, saying, "Please."

Nabi Khan took one from the packet and put it to his mouth. His hand was trembling.

"Nabi Khan, you've had a hard day. Relax, why don't you?"

Mr. Soleymaani lit his cigarette.

Nabi Khan then broke down and said, "*Agha*, I didn't do anything wrong! It was pen and paper, I didn't do anything wrong..."

Mr. Soleymaani nodded and with a slight smile, patted him on the knee, "I know."

Mr. Soleymaani then turned his head and saw that they had pulled up in front of the gated entrance to his house. He got out and said, "Goodbye."

Mr. Soleymaani closed the door, threw his cigarette to the ground, and started to walk away. Nabi Khan, who was still in the back seat, was pleading, "Agha, for God's sake, please...," but no one heard him.

The car drove off.

The two guards led Arash to a room. They made him sit on a chair and left him there. Because he was blindfolded, he purposefully listened for the two pairs of footsteps leaving the room. If nothing else, the time in isolation had improved his sense of hearing. The door shut, the dull sound of an ordinary wooden door he had not heard in months. He also knew he was near a window as he felt the warmth of the sunshine on his chest and part of his face.

After a while they came back and led him out of the room, into the hallway, and down a series of stairs. They were now more gruff with him, pushing him, and every now and then prodding him in the ribs with a baton. If he lost his balance and fell, they would laugh and say, "What's the matter with you, can't you even walk straight?"

He was thrown into the room and he heard the door close behind him. It had the hollow metallic sound of his own cell. But he had also heard the guards follow him in and knew this was not his cell. He did not move.

They, too, kept still, waiting for him to make the first move. Their patience tired more readily than his, and one of the guards finally yelled, "Get up!"

Arash was startled and his body jerked but he silently refused what they had asked him, not in order to disobey them but because he knew what was to come. He tried to curl up in a fetal position, the best way he could with his hands tied behind him and his feet fastened together.

"Get up you mother-fucking whore-monger!"

He did not budge. A string of verbal assaults was quickly followed by the first strike. Before he could even appreciate the sharp pangs coming from his chest, a slurry of blows followed.

The whip was brought out next. One lash followed the next, and soon his back was inflamed, covered with streaks of blood.

Towards the end they took turns, with one sitting out, resting on a chair, looking on while smoking a cigarette. When the guards started to get tired, one said, "It is time for the Apollo!"

By now Arash's blindfold had partly come off and he caught a glimpse of the strange contraption, shaped like a table that stood in the middle of the room. This was the famed Apollo. A helmet not unlike an astronaut's was placed on Arash's head. The sound of his own heavy breathing echoed in that small chamber. He could smell the fear of all those who had worn the helmet before him. One of the guards grabbed his feet. The other lifted him under his arms and they effortlessly carried his limp body over to the table and swung him onto it. Arash caught a glimpse of a small bronze plaque on the Apollo. It said, 'Made in the USA'. His arms and legs were unshackled only to be fastened to the table. A switch was flipped. The old engine, slow at first, gathered momentum with each rotation. The table began to shake as if it was about to take-off. Yes, they had not called it the Apollo without good reason. Arash could feel the mechanical hum vibrate through his entire body, especially his head. Then two heavy, metal rods at the end of the table (where his feet were situated) started to move back and forth. They, too, were slow at first, only lightly pressing the sole of one foot before retreating and letting the other rod do the same to the other sole. With each cycle they gained speed and strength. The slight pressing soon gave way to slaps which gave way to heavy blows. At its peak, Arash imagined a Herculean beast wielding a metal pipe, throwing all its energy into each blow, unwavering and untiring.

Meanwhile the guards worked on other parts of his body with whips, needles, and fire. At a certain point the pain became excruciating, but more or less constant. He did not feel the rods against his soles so much as the cumulative pain. His screams echoed in the helmet. He threw up several times, the vomit gathering around his neck and chin, a few drops trickling out of the helmet. He closed his eyes in an effort to become less claustrophobic. But the vibration sounded like jackhammers in his ears and, in the darkness, he was floating through space in an endless nauseating nightmare.

After what seemed like hours they stopped and removed the helmet. They asked for information, about Sir Buckley, about his contacts. He tried to talk, and although his tongue and lips were moving, no coherent words escaped his lips. They did not seem satisfied. Then one said, "So do you think we can torture now?"

They beat him more. When they saw that he was near death, they threw him back in the cell. Never would he have imagined that he would be so happy to come back to his solitary cell.

* * *

With the coming days many parts of his body hurt, parts he did not even remember being manipulated. His nose was broken as were a few ribs. It hurt to breathe, to live. He could not move a finger without pain.

But move he did. His thirst was so great that he crawled, bit by bit, dragging his battered body next to the door so he could turn in his empty tray for bread and water. He stayed in the same position for days as he only had enough energy to take a few sips of water. Everything else was a luxury he could not afford. He relieved himself where he was, soiling his clothes and the ground underneath.

Day 6

O Judge! Let us be frank with each other. I understand it all completely, now that I have had several days to think. I was naive and you caught me off-guard.

I had been in Evin for a month or two and was treated well. I became complacent and thought you had forgotten about me. After I wrote on that first day, I felt a sudden panic, as if someone was watching me, so I wrote a second version and began to destroy the first one. But before I could do so the guards took the pages away. There must be a hidden camera, or the person from whom I got the pen must have told someone.

After a while, the guards came back and blindfolded me. They took me to a different room where I was tortured. But I don't want to talk about that. All I will say is that I haven't even been able to hold a pen in my hand until today.

Now I am feeling a bit better. You see, I have nothing to hide. There are easier ways to obtain information than by torture. I will give you an account of all that has transpired during the past months, even more than I gave in the prior questionings. I know these pages will be read, and I know they will be used at my trial. My hands are still bruised and so it is painful to write. This will have to do for today.

Day 7

It is a new day. I am feeling better, my aches are diminishing. They have brought me food today but have forgotten the medicine.

Now it is time to write. The first day stands as it was originally written. Sir Buckley, once again, was not a spy so far as I know. He was just an unfortunate Iranian I met, a man who was stuck in transit for years because he was without a visa. I have nothing more to add to that. When I boarded the plane, the stewardess showed me to a first-class seat. She said it was courtesy of Sir Buckley. I never knew a plane ride could be so comfortable.

It was early in the morning when I arrived at Mehrabad, I think around 4 A.M., and still dark. Flying in, looking out the window, Tehran's lights below seemed like a field of glittering gold, without beginning or end.

The plane landed and we walked out onto the runway. I had finally arrived. All the strange feelings and worries of the past weeks were behind me. I must say that at that moment I truly felt I was home, in the midst of something comforting and familiar, regardless of the years that had gone by. I became very emotional and a few tears formed in my eyes, one or two falling to the ground.

We then boarded a bus to the main terminal. At immigration I ran into a bit of trouble. The officer asked, "Where is your exit visa?"

I said, "I don't have one."

He placed a stamp in my passport, looked at me curiously, and said, "In that case you can apply for one at —— building on ——."

I wrote all this down, even though I had come with the intention of staying. The rest of the airport procedures went on without hassle. I changed some of my dollars into tomans, picked up my bags, and walked towards the exit. Throngs of family and friends had gathered around the exit, eagerly looking past me to catch a glimpse of their loved ones. With all my close family in the West, there was no one waiting for me. I felt a twinge of sadness, but I didn't let it sink in.

I got into a cab, asking for the Hyatt Hotel. The streets were utterly empty. But I knew it was because of the night and that they would swell in the daytime. Images of Imam Khomeini were everywhere, all the more noticeable at night when the other distractions of the day were absent. All in all, the streets seemed peaceful, Imam Khomeini guiding our way. The driver pointed out the many new expressways that had been built since the Revolution. He dropped me off in front of the Hotel Evin. I didn't think too much of it as I thought this was the post-revolutionary name for the Hyatt.

The first few days I did not venture far from the hotel, mostly because of a bout of diarrhea. I absorbed all that was around me. I was especially intrigued by the newspapers. I read them all, liberal, conservative—it did not matter. Each side staunchly supported their party. How new and exciting it all seemed, the political rivalries and the newspaper commentaries.

Otherwise, I would watch television and eat my chelo kabob. *When my plate arrived, I would mix the rice with the melting butter, mashing in the yolk of a raw egg. Then I would break off a piece of tender kabob and eat it with a heaped tablespoon of rice, followed by a bite of raw onion. What I would do for a plate of that now!*

My window at the hotel faced the northeast and the mountains. I never did see Mt. Damavand, but I wasn't sure if it was the smog or the particular angle of view.

Such was the way I spent my first few days in Iran.

Day 8

They have not brought my medicine today, either. I left a note in my last food tray. O Judge! Please intercede. But they have yet to take all I have written away also.

The first time I had gone out for a walk was such an experience. I had a view of the streets below from my hotel room window, but actually walking amidst the crowd was quite a different experience. Everything was novel again, from the newspaper kiosk to the tea sellers yelling, "Cha-e! Cha-e!"

It was like in a dream. All around Persian was being spoken, not as in America, purposefully at a party or a store. Rather it was all around, bits of conversation in passing, the cries of the vendors, the high-pitched voices of the children. For this alone I had been dreaming for years.

The streets were jammed with cars and the sidewalks with pedestrians. The schoolgirls had their monteaus *on and traveled in packs on the sidewalks. The schoolboys in their white dress shirts also claimed the streets. The older ones crammed into cars, buses, and taxis. The stores were beginning to open, the owners pulling up the metal gates. I could not understand how anyone got anywhere in this city as it was so congested. I stopped and got several newspapers from one of the many kiosks. Then I went to a bookstore.*

I am sorry but I am not much inclined to write today.

Day 9

Still no medicine. My food, today, was also less than usual.

I feel a slight twinge in my chest, different from the pain that was getting better. I do not know if it is the disease, a bruised rib, or just my worrying.

When they had tortured him, Arash saw the men. They looked Iranian to him. Their lips were moving and he heard Persian being spoken. But he did not feel as if he was in Iran, or even Evin. How could they be Iranian, he thought, how could one Iranian do this to another? How could one human being do this to another? Pulling a trigger is a simple matter, oftentimes it does not even require any thought. But to torture someone for hours—what were they thinking as they delivered those blows?

His wounds slowly healed and when the new custodian placed the meal tray through the slot, he no longer jumped in alarm. The absence of the medicine, though, bothered him to no end. This was worse than any physical torture they could have come up with. When it became clear to Arash that this was not an oversight, not a mistake, he withdrew into himself.

Would it come back, he thought? The sores in his chest worried him. With these thoughts preoccupying him, he ceased to write in his journal. His days were spent lying on that cold ground, staring at the sky through the window.

Day 30

Is it day number thirty? I do not know, but it truly feels like No Ruz, *a day that is new. It has been, I believe, at least several weeks since I picked up this pen.*

Today a most extraordinary thing happened! I was lying in my dark cell, staring at the few rays of sunshine above, when a bird landed on my windowsill. I could not see the bird itself, but only its shadow on the opposing wall. In and of itself, this would have been a grand occurrence. But there was to be more. The shadow moved as the bird hopped about the ledge. Then its beak opened and a song was begun.

To me, who has only heard distant wailing and muffled loudspeakers over the last several months, or the friction of my own movements and the rattling of that blasted cough, the song that entered from the skies above carried the force of an avalanche. How can I ever truly describe it? It seemed to come from a far-off land, a place foreign to the way we live. So loud, melodious, and beautiful—it made me cry. I do not believe the Sirens ever sung so sweetly.

How delightful those few moments were, when I forgot all about my woes, when the bird's song carried me with it above and beyond my mortal body and the confines of my cell.

I lay still, without a movement, so as not to scare the bird away. Then the urge to cough came—a frightful urge that I fought with all my might, bearing down on my throat, stomach, and chest. Quiet, spasmodic contractions ensued until it finally forced its way out. It was a loud, ugly expulsion, bringing forth a thick yellow phlegm that I spat down the hole.

When I looked up the bird was gone.

The past few weeks have been particularly hard. I sank into a state of depression when I found out my medication was being withheld. I could not accept the fact that they wanted me to die. The fear that followed almost paralyzed me, so that when my fever finally announced itself, it was almost a relief.

At night I shiver and shiver; a rough cloth is all I have to keep me warm. By morning my clothes are drenched, as is the damp, cold stone underneath. And now the cough has returned.

O judge, who sit in your warm house, under your korsi, *with your seaghehs rubbing your feet and meeting all your sexual needs, handing you your tea and sugar cubes as you read this: Fuck you and all your friends with and without turbans. May you contract syphilis and AIDS. May your last days mirror the Shah's, wandering like a headless chicken in a strange and foreign land like all those you left homeless. I could never write freely anyway, knowing there was a chance to live.*

The weather is turning cold at the foot of these mountains, but there is still a bit of fat on these bones. As long as I have enough energy to place my empty plate through the slot on the bottom of the door, I will get a meal of bread and water. And with that, I can live and write a while longer. I only hope that the tiny bird comes once in a while to bring me news of the Tehran I knew.

* * *

Evin is at the foothill of these great mountains which stretch from the Caucuses to China. It is at the northernmost point of Tehran, where the need to build was superseded by the steep angle of this great rocky mass. Tehran will stretch and grow beneath me in all directions but north.

Outside of here, some semblance of normal life continues and the toil goes on, perhaps no different in effect from the centuries and millennia before when this land and its people were strangled by the Arabs, Mongols, Russians, and British—let us not forget the Americans—not to mention a long list of our own despotic and incompetent rulers.

There was a time, though, when it seemed that change was in the air, when the hope of fair rule captured the imagination. I was a boy of eleven or twelve then and in many ways did not appreciate the subtlety and underlying reasons of all that was happening. But the magnitude of the events was something that I deeply felt, leaving a strong imprint on my memories from then. The bit of sky that I see above reminds me of those days.

From the northern window of our apartment, Mt. Damavand was visible each and every day. The crisp snowcapped peak with the blue sky surrounding it was framed by our dining room window, making it our private painting. During the heady days of the Revolution, school was closed for days, sometimes even weeks. After the first such emergency closures, our teachers had given us photocopied packets of schoolwork so that we would not fall behind. Those first few days, Naazi and I celebrated our freedom, thinking it was a stroke of good fortune, an unexpected holiday, but soon we became bored with the monotony and it dawned on us that we were the furthest thing from being free.

Because of the danger, Naazi and I were not allowed to go outside and so were cramped in our tiny apartment for days on end. I remember having nothing to do but stare at Damavand, ever present and never changing. We tried to keep ourselves busy, but it was hard, day after day, to come up with new things to do in our two-bedroom apartment. Sometimes we would go out on our balcony and look at the comings and goings of our neighbor's chickens, whose lives, though monotonous like ours, seemed somehow more eventful.

We finally resorted to playing football indoors, knowing full well that it was forbidden. So dire was our situation that when I made the suggestion of playing football, a sport which Naazi had previously never showed any interest in, she received it quite enthusiastically. It was a matter of time, yes. No matter how many precautions we took such as placing pillows and blankets against the window and balcony door, no matter how much care we placed in each and every kick, there was bound to be one mishit ball or an unlucky bounce. It came from my foot, hitting the balcony door handle (one of the goal posts) dead on and bouncing back over my head and landing on the table, bowling over the vase, causing it to fall to the floor and shatter into many pieces. The rest of our day was ruined as we anxiously awaited our mother's return, that fateful moment when the front door would open. My mother usually would have given us a good yelling along with a stern punishment. To our surprise and delight, she did not seem to be the least put off by it.

In those early days, the people had become concerned with something larger than life. There was a feeling in the air—a longing of centuries, the smell of nah *with the first rains that announce the end of a long drought. It was the moment of still-water, when the outgoing tide ceases for an instant before the flow of water reverses, before the course of life would be changed forever. Everything else was forgotten as we huddled next to our radios at night, listening to the latest BBC news about the events unfolding on the streets.*

At night, if the weather was good, Naazi and I would take our bedding to the roof, staring at the stars before falling asleep. One night we heard the rumble of a tank as it went by. The entire building was vibrating back and forth, as if someone had taken it by the collar and given it a vigorous shaking. We thought it was an earthquake until we heard the roar of the massive engine and the clanking of its metal tracks. Other nights, sporadic machine-gun fire would surprise us like the occasional shooting star overhead.

One day I snuck out. I had to beg and plead with Naazi to keep the secret, not to tell our mother. She eventually gave in to the promise of some sweets. I put on my sneakers, a pair of white Adidas with green stripes. The great football players of the 1978 World Cup wore Adidas and so I had to as well. That year, Iran had made it to the World Cup, and even the tragic self-goal against Scotland could not quell my enthusiasm. A friend of the family who also had a love of sports had heard of a store that still had Adidas in stock, and so after weeks of fruitless searching, I bought this pair.

I went down the flight of stairs and opened the door to the street. The city stood before me as my prison of the last months quickly faded behind me. I had a couple of tomans in my pocket and my Adidas on my feet. I felt like the ancient kings who would disguise themselves to escape their own entourage, going out alone to catch a real glimpse of the city. I wanted to experience it all for myself: all that I had seen on the television, read in the newspapers, and heard about secondhand from my family.

It was early in the afternoon, on a bright and sunny day. Our neighborhood was uncharacteristically quiet, the way it used to be late at night. I could hear a lone crow cawing on a nearby tree. The cars lined the street just beyond the joob, *which had fast running water flowing downhill. Behind the* joob *was the sidewalk and then the walls that separated the houses and their yards from each other and the street. These walls were now filled with graffiti and slogans. "Death to the Shah" was the most common. Some of them had been sprayed over and over again by rival factions. They were all done in haste, lest anyone in authority see them. The drippings trailed down with gravity before becoming frozen in time.*

I sat by the side of the joob *for a minute, my legs forming a bridge from the sidewalk to the street. The clear water moved swiftly by, sparkling in the sun as it softly gurgled past. I grabbed a stick and put it into the water, dividing the stream in two, making the water splash up a bit to make my legs wet. There was nothing interesting, only a few plastic wrappers and an apple core bobbing by. Once I had seen a live mouse being swept away by the stream, frantically paddling, struggling to keep its head above water. I had chased after it for several blocks before the* joob *took the mouse underground.*

As I sat there, caught in the rhythm of the water, I saw a movement straight ahead of me. I looked up. It was the usual gang of stray dogs napping on the opposing sidewalk. They actually looked a bit better than usual, more meat on their skinny ribs. Their leader had golden fur and was big. His ears were pointing straight up and his eyes were fixed on me. We had been sworn enemies for years, but I left them alone. I think it was around this time that I began to feel sorry for them, or maybe it was that I had other plans. How cruel we were to those poor beasts. I will have to write about that later. In any case, I got up and walked towards the main road.

A five minute walk was all that was needed to get to Naaser Agha*'s store. The main road was just as quiet as our street. Once in a while a solitary car would drive by. I had never really seen our neighborhood as such, without any distractions, and I noticed many things for the first time. All of a sudden the trees that lined the* joobs *made themselves known. The houses could not be seen from the street, but the walls, each with fresh graffiti, became new landmarks.*

Soon, I was at the front of the tiny grocery store. Naaser Agha sold only the basics: milk products, canned goods, and packaged snacks. It was the last which attracted all the children of the neighborhood. Naaser Agha was always sitting behind the counter, a slightly portly man in his middle years, hair beginning to gray around the edges, wearing a pair of glasses and reading his newspaper while the short-wave radio played in the background. That day was like the others; as I walked in he looked up for a moment before looking at his newspaper again.

"Salaam Naaser Agha."

*This time he looked up and put away the paper. "*Bah-bah, *look at you, I didn't even recognize you. You haven't been here in a long time."*

"The uprising—"

"Ah yes, the uprising. Your mother still comes here often, but I haven't seen you. The schools have shut down, yes?"

I nodded yes and he continued, "That's a problem. How is this country to go on? And this is just the beginning. No one knows what will happen and no one is asking. When the regime changes like this, by force, anything can happen. The Tudeh, Mojahedin, Fadaiyan-e Khalgh, *or other fanatics—there are new ones popping up every day. Anyone can take control."*

I had heard the names of those groups many times, and

from each person I had heard something different, some in praise, others critical like Naaser Agha, so that I never knew what to make of those groups. When he saw me not answering, he smiled and said, "Well, what can I do for you today?"

"One Pofak *and one Kit Kat."*

He got these from underneath the glass counter and handed them to me. I thanked him and paid him the money. As I was leaving he said, "Listen, you had better go straight home. I just heard on BBC *that there are demonstrations again today."*

I waved to him and said, "Thanks, good-bye."

Now it all made sense. The demonstrations had emptied the streets. I put the Kit Kat I got for my sister in my pocket and opened the bag of Pofak *and put one in my mouth. Naaser Agha had given me just the information I was looking for. There was nothing to do but join the demonstration. I only had a vague idea of where I was going, but you did not have to be that old to understand that it was the South where all the trouble, or action, was. And to get to the South, all you had to do was follow the downward slope of any main street.*

I began walking and in no time found myself in areas I had never seen before. Those streets, like the ones around our neighborhood, were all but empty. I remember walking for a long time, easily a few hours, before strange things began to happen. I had been spotting more and more people in the streets, and it seemed that they were all walking toward the same destination. I followed them. At one point I began hearing the distant, rhythmic chanting. It was getting louder and louder with each step, and the closer we got, the larger our ranks swelled, like streams pouring into a river. Then suddenly the small street I was on came upon the main road, and in front of me was a sea of people, the size of which I had never seen before.

This mass extended in both directions as far as I could see, taking over both street and sidewalk. The noise was an incredible mixture of feet shuffling and voices chanting in unison. Those with the loudspeakers would shout out a slogan and the crowd would follow. There was anger and a painful discontent in their faces, in their voices. Some held handmade signs, others carried banners. They all looked so much older than I, but thinking of it now, they were mostly young adults, predominantly men. But I did see people of all ages, from men with graying hair and old women with chadors *to a few as young as myself. I took a few steps forward and at once was pulled into the current that was moving much faster than I was accustomed to walking. I kept up though, and was soon caught up in the excitement and frenzy, chanting slogans and shaking my fists in the air with the rest.*

After half an hour or so, the people in front of us stopped and everyone was pressed against each other. The chanting had also ceased and a brief, confused silence ensued. Then, without warning, gun shots were fired, much louder than the far-off ones I would hear from our rooftop. Suddenly, everyone around me was scrambling to get away, pushing and shoving in all directions.

I was lost amongst their screams and legs, struggling to keep my balance. I soon found myself on the frontline. There was no one between me and the soldiers across the street who were taking aim at the crowd. The soldiers were dressed in riot gear and armed with rifles.

A terror seized me and I could not get myself to move. I knew I should flee to safety like the others around me but I could not. My eyes were all that were moving as they haphazardly shifted from one scene to another. I only saw a few people by my side, the rest having escaped to the side streets. Shots were being fired, I could hear them ricocheting off the street and the walls of the buildings. I also heard the sound of glass breaking and the explosions of Molotov cocktails. There was blood on the asphalt, still liquid, not yet coagulated. There were many slumped on the ground or limping away. Their cries and groans were terrifying.

I saw one young woman, already with a gunshot to her arm and blood splattered on her face. She was holding her wounded bicep with one hand. As she turned to run away, our eyes met.

There was fear in her brown eyes, as there were in mine. She momentarily hesitated, perhaps wanting to come over to me, to save me. It was only for an instant, the pause, but now her image is forever frozen in my mind: the bleeding arm as it hung lifelessly from pain, the indecision in her eyes, and the attempted escape were all pulling her body in different directions. She was looking at me as a fresh bullet struck her in the back. She jerked forward with the impact, falling heavily, face down on the ground. I could not see her face anymore, her long hair was covering it. She twitched a few times and did not move again.

When I saw this, I regained my senses and jumped behind a man next to me who was throwing a Molotov cocktail at the soldiers. I remember hearing a loud scream and then everything became black.

When I came to, I was looking down the back of a man onto the asphalt. The man had gripped my two legs tightly to his own chest with his right hand. My waist was hooked on the man's shoulder and my upper body hung down his back. I kept quiet, trying to figure out what was happening as I bounced up and down with his every step. Then I noticed he was limping on an injured foot. The sight of his bloodstained pants scared me out of silence and I said, "Agha, Agha, let me down!"

He stopped, put me on the sidewalk and asked, "Are you alright?

Somewhat reassured, I looked at the man and said, "I'm fine. What happened?"

"I was shot in the leg and I fell back on you. Your head must've hit the ground because you were unconscious. I picked you up and took you away."

I felt my scalp with my hand and felt a bump in the back that hurt when I pressed on it. I said, "Thanks."

"Don't mention it. My name's Reza, what's yours?"

"Arash."

We started walking again. As I looked around I suddenly

realized I had no idea where in Tehran we were. I asked, "Where are we?"

"Near Tehran University."

"What are you going to do about your leg?"

"I have a friend in the medical school. I'm going there. Do you want to come to get checked out too?"

"Sure," I said confidently, trying to act older, while in reality I was still scared.

We started to walk. Although walking with vigor, Reza looked tired. His face was unshaven and his hair greasy. Those were the days of agitation and nights without sleep. Even I, who was on the periphery, would stay up late listening to the radio and the discussions of my mother and her friends.

I was looking at Reza's wounded leg with a bloody rag tied around it, when I asked, "Does it hurt?"

"Oh yes."

"Listen, when you picked me up, did you see a lady next to us that was on the ground?"

He turned to me with a strange and inquisitive look, asking, "There were so many injured, why?"

"I saw her get shot."

He shrugged and said, "No, I don't remember seeing anyone nearby. She's probably alright. Look at my leg, see the blood. Stop for a moment."

We both stopped. Reza turned around and I did the same. There was a trail of blood along the sidewalk. He pointed to it and in an emotional and emphatic tone said, "Look behind you. Do you see that trail of blood—this is my blood, drop by drop on the sidewalk. This is my blood for this country, for overthrowing the Shah! Many of us have died, and many more will."

Somehow his explanation was not consoling. We continued to walk in silence.

Soon we were in front of an unassuming apartment building. He rang the buzzer. The voice on the other end said tersely, "Who is it?"

"Jules Verne."

The door opened and we walked inside and up the stairs. I was now feeling a bit of excitement. I knew exactly what was happening. I had seen this in movies and read about it in books. I had even experienced it only a few weeks before. One day at home I decided to call my friend Payam whom I had not talked to in weeks. I must have dialed the wrong number because a man whose voice I did not recognize answered the phone.

I asked, "Is Payam there?"

The man on the other end said, "We are meeting at the cinema tonight, 9 P.M." He hung up as soon as his sentence was finished. He had given me the message.

When Reza and I got to the apartment, he knocked in a peculiar way, and the door suddenly opened. There was a man on the other side. I looked past him and into the apartment. I was disappointed. I was expecting the exotic flat of a spy, not a dingy, run-down apartment with the curtains pulled and a mess of cloths and papers on the floor.

"Who is he?" the man demanded, eyeing me suspiciously.

"This is Arash. And this," he said pointing to his friend that looked nothing like the hero I imagined, "is Hossein."

Hossein nodded and shifted his gaze toward Reza's bloody leg, suddenly exclaiming, "What happened to you?! Why are you standing there?! Come in, come in! Let's go to the kitchen!"

We stepped inside and walked towards the kitchen.

"I was at the demonstration. The Shah's soldiers fired on us again. I was shot in the leg, falling back on Arash, knocking him unconscious."

"Please have a seat. Let me get the scissors."

Hossein lit a candle and placed it on the table before he left the room. We sat at the table and Reza looked at me with an embarrassed smile, as he was the one in need of help now. Hossein came back a minute later, walking swiftly to and fro, getting all the things he needed. He put the scissors to the flame and then went toward Reza.

Reza motioned for him to stop and asked, "You want to cut off my pants?"

"Yes."

"But I only have a few pairs of pants, why can't I take them off?"

"As you wish, but this is what we usually do, it's easier."

Hossein helped him take off his pants, though with some difficulty and pain. He then took a towel, wet it in a bowl with water, and gently rubbed the blood, both dried and fresh, off his leg. Then he stuffed the wounds with cotton saying, "You're lucky, the bullet has exited the back, you can see the two holes in your pants. Now do you have feeling over the entire leg and foot?"

"I think so."

"Let me see you wiggle your toes."

He wiggled his toes and Hossein said, "Good, now let me examine your leg."

After a few more minutes of examination, Hossein stood up pleased and said, "You're very lucky indeed. No major nerves or arteries were in the path of the bullet. I don't think you need to go to the hospital. I can suture this up here."

He then got out the suturing kit. He proceeded to take the cotton out from the wounds and suture the holes shut. I was fascinated. It was just like when my grandmother had sewn clothes, but this was raw flesh. Reza grimaced and clenched his teeth the whole time.

Hossein looked up at him and said, "Sorry, I don't have any anesthetic, so it might hurt a bit."

After fifteen minutes, he had tied the last knot. "Now, tomorrow I want you to come by the hospital so I can give you a shot."

"Thanks, now can you take a look at my friend. He was out for a long time."

Hossein sat down on the chair facing me, keeping his eyes on me while speaking to Reza, "I didn't say anything when you brought him here, but you know I'm only a doctor for the organization."

I looked over to Reza for some support, but he was busy putting his pants back on. Hossein now addressed me in a scornful way, asking, "What do you know about me, or us?"

"Leave him alone, he's only a boy," Reza said, as he shuffled closer to us.

"Do you know what a Communist is?" he demanded, looking at me.

I did not answer him.

He asked again, only louder, "Answer me, do you know what a Communist is?"

I shook my head.

"Hossein, leave him alone," Reza said, moving even closer to us.

With each new question Hossein was raising his voice louder.

"We believe in the equality of all people. The worker should have just as much power as any other. What do you say to that?"

By now my anger at the interrogation was mixed with a bit of fear, but I still did not answer as I was confused and had no idea what he was talking about.

He asked, "If I were to take your shoes and give them to a poor boy, one who doesn't have any shoes, would you agree?"

He had now asked me a question that I not only understood, but could give the answer to as well. "But then what would I wear?" I spat back at him.

"Bourgeois! You see Reza, only concerned about I. Let him go back to North Tehran. When the Revolution comes—"

Reza grabbed him by the shoulder, pulling him from the chair, and said, "Hossein! Come to the other room. I want to talk to you."

They hastily walked out of the room and I remained in the kitchen. Their voices were peaked with emotion, trying in vain to keep their conversation private. I heard everything they said and had a partial view of their faces from where I was seated.

"What right had you to bring him here? You could jeopardize all of us!"

"Can't you see he's harmless. He's just a boy, not even ten. Give him a break—he's shaken up. He saw someone killed today, Hossein, a girl at the demonstration—right next to us. After I picked him up, I went over to her, she was dead. He was asking about her."

"Anyone we know?" he asked, his expression softening for a moment.

"A familiar face, I think she may have been in one or two of the meetings last year, but I had seen her on campus."

"At least she wasn't part of the Tudeh*."*

"How can you say that?" Reza said passionately, "She gave her life!"

There was a silence, then Hossein continued, "To be on the safe side, we should get his name and address, in case he tells someone."

"No! There is no way I'm doing such a thing. I will not let you do it either. Why do you want to scare him more? He could be your own brother. He wouldn't have known a thing if you hadn't opened your mouth. Anyway, he's never even been in this neighborhood or even near the university. I'll take full responsibility."

Reza came back in the kitchen and cheerlessly said, "Come on, let's go."

We walked silently out of the apartment and into the street.

"I'm sorry about Hossein. He's a reliable friend, but sometimes he can be too…"

I knew Reza had wanted to say "coldhearted," but he stopped himself, looking for a different word.

I said, "Don't worry, I won't tell anyone."

When we got to the main road, he flagged down a taxi. We shook hands and he handed me a few tomans for the ride.

"Good-bye."

"Good-bye."

Driving back in the Taxi, the streets were once again filled with people and traffic. I sat dejected in the back seat, looking at the scenes drifting past. In the morning how I had looked forward to seeing the bustling city that had been hidden from me during the past months. The graffiti slogans did not interest me now, nor did the stores which had reopened or the people that filled the sidewalks. Tehran had lost its luster.

I was glad I had beaten my mother home. As soon as I entered the house Naazi asked, "Where's my chocolate?"

I pulled out the package of Kit Kat, by now melted, and gave it to her. "Why is it so squishy?" Naazi complained.

"The uprising," was the half-truth I came up with, not wanting to get into the long and uncomfortable explanation.

That day I had gotten my first true taste of the Revolution. I still did not understand many things: the Tudeh, *Communism and shoes, Hossein's attitude, the secrecy. But I had also seen blood that needed no explanation and the face of death that has yet to leave me. That night I pulled the covers over my head but I could not rid myself of her image. I was scared and also touched with a strange sadness, silently crying myself to sleep.*

* * *

Days, weeks, and months passed. I stayed in on most days and no longer minded as much. With nothing to do, we would listen to the radio and sing along with the revolutionary songs. My favorite from that period went, "Allah Allah Allah, La Allah-ha-ill-Allah*!"*

Other times I would sit at the table and stare at Damavand. It was during this period that we moved from our apartment to a house. We looked forward to the quiet times when we could go back to school. There were some highlights, though.

The day the Shah left was a day that stands out clearly in my mind from the blurry days and weeks that surrounded it. The weather itself was the example of Tehran at its finest: sunny but not hot, the endless blue sky above. I was at a friend's house. He lived in one of the then modern sky rises, tens of floors above the ground. His mom had made us salad olovieh for lunch. We were eating our food and watching TV, when the program was suddenly interrupted, replaced by an excited reporter who said that the Shah of Iran had left the country. Then we saw the images of the Shah at the airport, and the ceremony surrounding the boarding of the airplane.

We grabbed each other and cheered. My friend yelled, "Mom! Mom! The Shah is leaving!"

The news had spread rapidly. Almost instantly we heard the noise of a multitude of honking cars. We ran to the balcony and looked across at Tehran. I saw the tiny cars moving in the streets below. Their honking was the same as those in the time of a wedding: short, repetitive, and joyous. I could not make out any of the people, but I knew, and they knew, that the Shah was gone—that was all that mattered.

We took to the streets. People were singing and dancing. Grown men were crying. Everywhere total strangers were congratulating, even hugging each other. Everyone was saying, "The Shah has left! The Shah has left!" We were shouting it, we were living it. Great things were to follow, anything was possible. Never had I or have I since seen anything like it.

The next great event, of course, was Khomeini's return. I saw this on the television also. It was treated with as much importance, but it did not feel the same way to me. Khomeini waved as he came out of the plane and slowly descended the steps. From far away he looked weak, an old man who could have been anyone's grandfather. It seemed as if he had trouble enough walking a short distance as he cautiously took one step after another. But a close-up of his face revealed an altogether different person. It was the look in his eyes, a steely expression that would never change, that we would all get used to. It was stern and dour, powerful and self-assured, and no clear emotion was discernable. I had heard the name here and there, on the radio or in the slogans, but did not know who he was at the time. I turned off the television.

Even before Khomeini's return from exile, the human cost was mounting. During one of our school's few open days, a classmate of ours had found a live shell behind some bushes in the schoolyard and had blown off part of his hand. We were then given safety instructions on how to identify bullets, shells, and grenades and the consequences of playing with them.

With the coming days, the newspapers carried the names and sometimes the pictures of those executed the previous day. Usually, one would see a number of bloody corpses lined up on the ground. I would read the captions to see if any famous people had been killed.

The picture of the freshly executed Nasiri, the head of the SAVAK, *was one such person. His renowned cruelty garnered him a front page photo all to himself. I have no doubt that the Apollo used to torture me was a relic from the* SAVAK. *Anyway, Nasiri was slumped on the ground, dead eyes gazing skyward, a pool of blood around his head. Some, when they leave this world, cause more joy than grief, no matter how they meet their end.*

One night, my uncle came to our house and took me with him. It was rather later at night and he said he was going out for a drive with his friends. We drove through the quiet streets of Tehran. After some time, we parked. A few minutes after we got out of the car and started to walk, he pointed to a building and said, "That's the American Embassy, where the hostages are."

From the powerful position of a queen on the chessboard, advisor and protector of the king, these Americans had been reduced to mere pawns in an internal power struggle. Their invisible controller's shield now gone, they were dragged down to our world, the Third World, subject to the rules of the street.

Though the West considers the hostage-taking a senseless act of barbarity, I completely understand why they did it. When you feel that you, the mouse, have been batted around by the paws of a cat for centuries, when only a quarter of a century earlier the CIA *staged a coup to replace a fledgling democracy with a dictator, when only a few months prior President Carter called the same dictator a great friend of America while touting his Human Rights campaign worldwide, when this same dictator was using American know-how and blessing to torture, imprison, and rob his own people, and when you feel powerless and expendable but the oil under your feet is not, when you know there is no recourse for all of the above…then it all makes sense.*

I really believe that the storming of the embassy by the students was a cry to the world, that we are people too, that our lives do matter. The hostage-takers held the personnel of the embassy as agents responsible for the actions of their government. That many of the hostages were cogs in a machine whose history and function they did not fully know or understand was a point lost on the students. They even naively thought that the American people would rally behind them. What happened next, the transformation of that emotional outburst into a long political ordeal, should be credited to the shrewdness and savvy of Khomeini.

Looking at the wall surrounding the embassy, the world of those hostages was as far away from me as I from them; we had our own problems to deal with. We could not see over the embassy's outlying wall that stretched for a whole block, but the gates were manned by armed men. These sights were now commonplace. Everywhere the komitehs *were popping up, usually set up in confiscated houses or mansions. There was one right next to our house.*

Last night Arash had a difficult time falling asleep. All he could think about was the Revolution and all that happened afterwards. He knows he will not be able to stop thinking about it until he can write it down. He would have written last night but there are no lights here, as his cell darkens with the night. And by the time he was tired enough to sleep, his cough started again. But he was happy anyway, as he has not had a fever in several days.

Day 31

Our komiteh *was situated on the corner of Bahar Street, in a confiscated house that had belonged to a rich businessman. I had never known who the previous owner was, as the entrance to his house was not visible from the street where we used to play. The walls surrounding the mansion were not particularly high, but I think the landscaping was done to the effect that it was hard to see it from most vantage points. Some of the houses in the neighborhood had a limited view of that house, but ours was not one of them. The* komiteh *had placed barbed wire and several loudspeakers above the walls. I took comfort in the fact that if we could not see them, then they could not see us either.*

Outside the main entrance, a pasdar *in camouflage, armed with a Kaloshnikov, stood guard behind a waist-high wall of sandbags. Occasionally, the* pasdar *would leave his post and pace the alley alongside the* komiteh. *The gate was usually closed but as they entered and left, I could sometimes catch a glimpse of the compound inside. Not that there was much to see. A few revolutionary banners in the courtyard, a large grassy lawn, and the main house behind it. What went on inside I did not want to know.*

No matter how bad the situation, one always tries to hold on to the way of life one is accustomed to. It was the same with my mother. She liked the music of her youth, she liked certain kinds of books that were popular among the circles she frequented, and when in the company of friends she would occasionally sip on a vodka and orange juice. She told me that there came a day for her, though, when to hold on any longer would have been foolish, much like the dead Pompeian who carried his earthly goods straight to the grave.

The stories were all around—so and so was taken to the komiteh *or somehow disappeared and was never seen again. These stories had worried her but not to the point of actually changing anything. The search of our neighbor's house, however, had frightened her to the point of action. There had been no reason, she thought, they were not political, nor were they Zoroastrian, Bahai, Armenian, or Jewish. That day she made up her mind. My father, she had thought, would have taken action much sooner.*

The vodka was poured down the drain, and later that day my uncle and I gathered the empty vodka bottles, any questionable books, and all the cassette tapes of Googoosh and Haydeh. We drove several hours into the desert, and when sure no one was coming from either direction, flung them into the sands, and quickly drove back to Tehran. We had one last tape of Haydeh that we listened to in the car on the way back, taking care to throw it in the joob *before returning home. As events like these had become routine, I no longer asked questions about them.*

When we came back, there was another assignment waiting for me. My mother gave money to Naazi and I to buy a picture of Khomeini. The two of us trod off to the main roundabout near our house, happy in that we had a task to accomplish. We did not have to go far. Quite a business had sprung up almost overnight and the pictures could be bought almost anywhere. The man we approached was standing on the street corner and was selling two such photos. He was yelling, "We've got photos, photos of the Ayatollah! Get your photos here! Savab dareh! Savab!*"*

Naazi went up to the dealer and asked, "Agha, how much are those?"

"Let's see, they both are the same price, fifteen tomans each,

but because you are such young revolutionaries, I'll give it to you for ten."

"OK."

"Which one do you want?"

Naazi and I looked at the two photos. One was a close up of Khomeini's profile. He was looking slightly downward, no doubt at the masses he was addressing. The other was a staged photo, a full figure view, with Khomeini standing in a garden facing the camera.

Naazi whispered in my ear, "Akhh... he sure is ugly, which one do you want to live with?"

"The one where you can see him standing so we don't have to look at that face every day," I whispered back giggling.

"But the garden, what a shame, a scene this pretty."

"Children, children, I've never seen anyone so excited at buying the Ayatollah's picture," the peddler said, "There's others waiting—come on now, tell me which one do you want?"

Naazi pointed to the one in the garden and handed him ten tomans. Once home, we put it in a frame and placed it in such a manner that this would be the first face greeting anyone who entered the house.

* * *

One day news came that Mehrabad Airport in Tehran was bombed by Iraq, and that was the beginning of the long war with Iraq. In no time, boys were running away from home to join the army, the sweet promises of martyrdom, heaven, and their very own machine-guns whispering in their ears.

My bus stop was across the street from the komiteh. *Consequently, each morning I had the pleasure of seeing the same* pasdar. *There was another boy in our neighborhood by the name of Amir who happened to be a classmate of mine, and so we would wait for the bus together.*

After several weeks of the same morning routine, the pasdar *tried to befriend Amir and I. The* pasdar *seemed a lot older than us, perhaps close to twenty. He had short black hair and a thin beard, though his face still had boyish features. At first, he would ask only about our school and the classes we had. Then, as the days went by, he began asking about our families and other aspects of our lives. Even before we told him anything, he seemed to know a lot about us. I never felt comfortable around him and it showed. Amir, though, was enthusiastic, in awe of the green uniform, the machine-gun, the power. One day the* pasdar *took off his machine-gun and placed it in our hands. He asked, "How do you like it?"*

"It's great." I said, perhaps a bit flatly, far from convincing.

Amir said, "Wow! Can I fire it?"

"I couldn't let you fire it here. Maybe you can come to the komiteh *sometime after school. You know there are a lot kids your age volunteering to fight. How old are you anyway?"*

At the same time we blurted out eleven and thirteen. The pasdar *laughed and said, "That is the difference between you two. You told me you are in the same grade." The* pasdar *pointed to him and smiled, "One lies about his age to serve Islam," then he pointed to me and frowned, "the other lies to serve himself."*

That night I told my mother about the episode and Amir's growing fascination with the pasdars. *She walked over to his house and had a talk with his mother, who was one of her friends. The following week we had a new bus stop, for reasons unbeknownst to Amir, and soon he forgot about the* komiteh.

More changes were ahead. All the schools that were funded privately were forced to close and only the state-sponsored ones remained. Previously, I had been attending one of the co-ed French-speaking schools, where both French and Persian were taught. Now I went to the all-boys school close to our house. The war brought on shortages of oil, gas, and food. With the scarcity of heating oil, hot water and a heated house became things of the past. During the winter we would wear our heavy coats and sweaters indoors. At night, all three of us would huddle under the electric korsi *as it snowed outside. And once a week we would go to the public baths for a hot shower. The decline in hygiene brought on an epidemic of lice in the schools, and all the boys were forced to shave their heads.*

The schools themselves were a well-intentioned social experiment. Children from all walks of society were required to attend the same schools. In reality there were only two groups: those whose parents were well off prior to the Revolution and who were now disenfranchised (the relatively new and growing middle class of the 60s and 70s and the old upper class), and those of the working and lower classes, those who theoretically had gained most from the Revolution. The two groups did not mingle with each other, and their group significantly outnumbered ours. Manners of speech, clothes, even experiences were vastly different. Only on the football field did we join, usually on opposing teams.

During recess I remember seeing the kids measuring their heights against the wall. They would take turns marking the wall with a piece of chalk, seeing who was tall enough to join the army. Thus, those who were tallest were the most respected. It was these same boys who would be used to clear the mines from the battlefield. It is said that when they sent them (young boys, goats, donkeys, and other animals) to do this work, after the first wave of explosions the animals would run back in fear, but the boys, armed with plastic keys, would still go bravely forth, being blasted to pieces while racing each other towards a heaven they each held a key for.

The first order of the day at school was the warm-up exercises. In between various stretches and calisthenics we were required to shout revolutionary slogans, fists raised in the air, repeating what our headmaster called out from behind the loudspeaker:

Death to America!
Death to Israel!
Marg Bar Monafeghin: *Carter, Sadat, O-Begin!*
Na Sharghi Na Gharbi: Jomhoorieh Islami

These slogans, which I had repeated faithfully and with such glee just a year or two ago, now rang false.

The first few weeks of the new school year were utter chaos, with no one knowing what class to go to or what time anything took place. I noticed that none of the teachers took attendance during the morning exercises so I made a habit of going for a long morning walk prior to my first class of the day. It took several weeks before they caught me. I was brought before the headmaster. I apologized profusely, stating that it was true, I was several minutes late to begin with, but then I was the witness to a most unfortunate accident, etc. He seemed distracted and overwhelmed by his new appointment. He was irritated at my intrusion on his work and he didn't know whether to believe me or not. But in the end he gave me the benefit of the doubt and sent me off with only a warning.

One day was dedicated to the burning of heretical books. The event was to take place after school, and various announcements and preparations were made during the preceding days. Throughout the day of the event, all foreign books, those not written in Persian or Arabic, and all books considered not in line with Khomeini's Islam were gathered and placed in a pile in the schoolyard. I recognized some as children's books I had read before. Attending this event was not formally required but was expected of the students. Because of the unfortunate 'morning walk' incident, I knew that I couldn't take any more risks, for a while anyway.

By the time I got there, the bonfire was already lit and the chanting had begun. I raised my fists in the air and joined the chorus of chants. Some of the kids were jumping over the fire like it was Charshanbeh Suri. *I stayed until the first few kids started to leave. I still remember seeing the smoke and ashes rising over the school wall as I walked home.*

Perhaps the most odious task of the day was the mandatory noon prayer. The entire school body had to congregate in a room barely able to hold a fraction of us. Before entering, we had to take off our shoes. Once inside, we had to stand in neat rows and pray.

The stench in that room was nauseating, filled with the smell of dirty socks, feet, and the body odor of a hundred prepubescent boys. It was especially bad when prostrated, when the sight and smell of the feet in front of me were almost touching my nose.

After several days of this torture, a friend and I devised a plan. We befriended our Koran teacher, a soldier who had just returned from the war. His class consisted of Koranic lessons, the fundamentals of Arabic, and updates on the latest troop movements on the front. Each day after class (which was luckily right before noon) we would stay behind and ask a few questions. Our eagerness was not false, it was simply displaced. That repulsive smell and the joy we took in escaping it, were the catalysts for asking questions about an otherwise boring subject. Our questions became more and more sophisticated with time, so that finally we had private, extra tutorials during the noon prayer. If time permitted we would pray with our teacher in the classroom. If there was not an opportunity to pray, it meant we were even more successful, and all the happier. After school we would laugh and slap each other on the back, not believing what we had got away with.

I actually hated my religion teacher. He reminded me of the pasdars *in our neighborhood: he had the same haircut and beard, the same camouflaged uniform—all that was missing was a machine-gun. He specifically resembled the one with whom I had a few run-ins.*

One day, while playing with our toy guns with the neighborhood kids, the pasdar *left his post and started to walk toward us. Even in our game, with all its careless laughter and jesting, we were distinctly aware of his presence. When he began to walk towards us, we automatically stopped our game, freezing in place, waiting to see what he wanted.*

He motioned for me to come to him. I had no choice but to obey. He met me halfway. The pasdar, who was much taller than I, looked down on me and scornfully asked, "What are you doing?"

Already feeling uneasy, I pointed the plastic gun behind me and said, "We were just playing with the other boys."

When I looked behind me, the alley was utterly empty. The kids had all run away. An empty, sinking feeling entered my stomach. With one hand he grabbed my shirt collar, with the other he took the muzzle of his machine-gun and shoved it against my neck, demanding, "How do I know that the gun in your hand isn't real?"

I was too scared to answer, to give the wrong answer. I had been avoiding his eyes, staring at his boots, when he shouted, "Look at me!"

I raised my eyes and saw a twisted smile, his piercing eyes locked on mine. "I could pull the trigger right now, and no one could do anything. Not your mom, not your uncle. No one!"

He held me there for a few moments and then suddenly loosened his grip and walked away. I heard his receding footsteps but dared not move or even look in his direction for minutes afterwards. Tears were streaming down my face.

After a few minutes I slowly walked away. I imagined he was standing at his post, resting his machine-gun on the sandbags, taking aim at my back, waiting and waiting until I was just around the corner, waiting for the moment when I thought I was free. Then he would pull the trigger and I would be shot like the young woman the Shah's soldiers killed. Each step was filled with this fear and those horrible thoughts. The last few steps were excruciating. I could not hold out any longer, and so without another thought, I sprang around the corner and ran to our house.

I was too scared to tell anyone what had happened and stayed in the yard for hours, happy to be within the confines of those four walls, our little bastion. With my back against the wall, the grass and the trees of the yard were in front of me. Beyond the walls, only the sky was visible, as the most menacing building in our neighborhood, the komiteh, *was safely behind me.*

Day 32

Ah, yes, there is nothing to send you reminiscing like a good pasdar *story. After writing those last words I put my pen down and went back to that alley on that day, to the exact spot by the wall, the uncomfortable bulge in my neck—all of it. How I hated him then. I could imagine no one I would have liked to have roughened up more. If only I was bigger, I thought, or if I could become invisible—then I would show him. But when I think of it now, I wonder if he knew any better. He was probably just back from the war and had seen many horrors. In me he saw a spoiled rich kid who did not understand the world, living a good life while those like him suffered. He was no doubt right. He did not pull the trigger and for that I am grateful, and because of that there is still hope.*

This reverie of mine was interrupted by a mosquito, yes a tiny little mosquito! I heard the high-pitched buzzing getting closer and closer. Then my eyes caught it as it hovered around me and landed on my arm. It swiftly got to work, inserting its needle to draw out the blood.

With one swift stroke I struck him dead, both our bloods smeared against my arm. I have been thinking about this ever since. There must have been a brief moment when my hand was pressed against its pinned and paralyzed body, when its blood-filled stomach swelled, bulging out to the limit of its tensile strength before bursting its contents onto my arm. That is the same moment she saw me before she was struck with the fatal bullet. That is the moment where I find myself now.

And why, I thought to myself, did I kill that poor bastard? Had he not a life of his own, filled with the infinite problems of mortality? If I am to die, then why not let him feed off me to extend his own life? Am I just a mosquito being squashed by the Akhounds, *or even worse, being brushed aside by the hands of time?*

At times I can only think of this death. It is then that a sinking feeling enters my body, a silent terror that stays for most of the day. Many days I wake with this despair. Once it has set in, it is paralyzing. I cannot think normally or even muster the energy to write.

From time to time, if it is a cloudless day and the rays of the sun come almost straight down, I can catch a glimpse of myself in the bowl of water. Even then it is only a dim outline. My bushy beard would make me look like a Hezbollahi *if it weren't for the long and unruly hair on my head. But even the beard can no longer hide my hollow eyes and gaunt face. I am not being fed enough, my medicine is being withheld. I have completely lost track of the days. The only certainty is that of death approaching, and at times, during the past weeks, the knowledge of it has been too much, making me depressed for days on end, preferring the darkness of my thoughts to the light above.*

Other times, like now, I can think about it quite detachedly. I am to join my other, the mosquito. When I die they will deny me a Moslem burial. They will not even find out for days or weeks afterwards, by which time I will be food for the rats, roaches, and other vermin. I will die a Zoroastrian death in this dakhmeh. *That suits me as well, as our forefathers were Zoroastrian and I always had an unusual affinity towards fire.*

I know such thoughts are not becoming of a good Moslem, but it is a bit late for that. How different my fate if I had been a believer. My grandparents prayed daily. My mother's uncle, himself, had been a mullah! He never trusted this government, and believed that religion had no place in politics. My mother had been less religious than her parents, believing in the basic tenets but not one to pray every day. I was destined to become even less religious than her.

The brutality of the Shah and Khomeini was the nail in the coffin, but I think this seed of religious doubt was instilled in me prior to the Revolution, when all seemed quiet and the people prosperous, high off the early Seventies oil boom.

Our family had gone on vacation in Shomal, visiting some

friends in Babol, situated south of the Caspian Sea, laying in the verdant valleys north of the Alborz Mountains. How I always loved going there, and almost better than the vacation was the journey itself. I would spend hours looking out the window as our car weaved its way through the gently rolling hills and rice fields. Every happening along the way to the beach was an adventure, from lunch at roadside chelo kabobi *to the Soviet radio stations we'd pick up on our car radio.*

That day in Babol I spent playing football with my family friend and one of the neighborhood children. Naazi was back at the house, playing with a girl her own age. As there were only three of us, we had a goalie, a defender, and a forward. We played on the paved street that stretched for several blocks. The forward would try to get past the defender and then attempt to shoot a goal. If he was successful we would rotate positions.

It was a beautiful day, sunny and mild, not even a hint of a cloud or a drop of rain as is typical of the North. As we played, we noticed a child in the distance, down the street. He was looking at us. The part of the street where he was standing was desolate, as this was a new development and the lots surrounding him were empty. Just beyond, there was the turnoff to a much larger street, with a median barrier down the middle and two lanes going each way.

In the midst of our game, I would periodically glance at the kid, but he did not budge. Had he come closer we would have invited him to play, rounding off our number to four, the minimum needed to play a decent game. He kept his distance like a street dog, and he was so far away that his features were barely discernable.

After a goal by one of the players (against me, the goalie), the ball rolled down the street, staying in the middle. The ground there was so flat that the ball kept rolling a long way in the direction of the boy. We waved and called to him to kick our ball back, expecting that the kid would either dribble or kick the ball back and join our game.

When the ball reached his feet, he very naturally picked it up, turned around, and started to run away from us, crossing the median and the street in the heavy traffic. The three of us chased after him, crossing the busy street without so much as a moment's hesitation, dodging the honking cars as they went past. I had a head start as I was the closest to the ball. I saw his figure dart into an alley ahead of us. When I turned the corner, I saw him make another turn. From behind me they were saying, "Where did he go? Where did he go?"

We kept running in pursuit and I just caught a glimpse of him entering a doorway, swiftly shutting the door behind him.

The three of us came to a stop in front of the wooden door, catching our breath for a few moments before we knocked. Until then, I had not noticed that we were running in the ghetto. The tight streets were unpaved and covered with dirt and gravel. The walls around the houses were made out of mud and straw. The puddles we had dodged whilst running were full of filth, breeding flies and mosquitoes.

My friend knocked on the door and we waited in anticipation. When the door opened, an old man stood in front of us. He was poor and was wearing faded clothes. He had a scruffy white beard and a small black cap on his head.

*He looked a bit surprised but said, "*Salaam Aleykum, *how are you doing? Please, please come inside."*

We replied Salaam and stepped into the tiny courtyard, ready to plead our case. It was small, without even a hoez. *Various tools and a wheelbarrow were stored in the courtyard. A leaky faucet had made the ground we were standing on wet, and the only vegetation in the yard was a few weeds which had sprung up below the faucet. Behind the old man was a woman in a black* chador *quietly staring at us.*

"What can I do for you?" the man asked.

"Someone took our football. Is there a kid here?"

He looked at the three of us for a moment and then nodded to his left. We had not even seen the boy. He was standing by the side of the building, just around the corner, and only partially visible. His back was towards us.

"Mahmood," he said looking over to the boy, "come here."

The boy did not move, keeping his back toward us.

"Mahmood, do you have their ball?" asked the man kindly, as if asking him a routine question.

Without a word Mahmood slowly turned around. Taking a small sidestep, he was now in full view. I saw our ball in his hands. His fingers were short and stubby. Then I looked up at his face. It was grotesque—the normal architecture seemed to have dissolved, replaced by bulbous growths jutting out of the most peculiar places. His nose itself had fallen off. From behind this fleshy mass peered two ashamed eyes gazing at the ground, shoulders drooping with the ball held dejectedly.

After the initial shock wore off, before he could extend his hand to give the ball back, in unison, all three of us turned in silence and ran out of the courtyard. We were terrified, never having seen anything like it. In the bazaar, I had once seen a disfigured fetus floating in a glass jar full of formaldehyde, but the boy standing in front of us was even more frightening as he was living and breathing, occupying the same space as us.

Heading out the doorway, I heard the ball drop to the ground, bouncing in place, each time softer and closer to the ground. We ran back all the way to our safe, familiar environment.

Thinking of it now, how ill he must have been. He had an enormous head start on us, but we easily managed to catch up to him. He must have known this as he ran away, that no matter how hard he tried, his every step was slower than ours. And this fear of being caught was only compounded by the fear of his inevitable rejection. And they both were to come to fruition when we knocked on his door.

I know we were children then, but I sometimes wish we had stayed, and wonder what would have happened if we had not run away, but instead asked him to play with us. I wish we could have seen his human eyes rather than feed the flames that burned his flesh and soul.

I felt sorry for him afterwards, and I could not understand how such a God that my grandmother talked about could allow such an atrocity. With the coming years, soon the very idea of God became so questionable that only faith, not logic, could save it. But I was not inclined that way.

That afternoon brought a glimpse of the world of poverty, pain, and disease that had been hidden from us, nay most of the Iranian middle and upper classes. The Revolution had to come, there was no doubt about it. For a brief moment it gave power to the poor, at least to those who joined the revolutionary ranks. It is unfortunate that this was not coupled with any education or substantial vision. That word "unfortunate" is too kind and detached a word, implying there was an effort or that those in power did not know better. In reality, all that was in place was the zeal for power that has left us with the chaos of today. And so in the end, some have risen and some have fallen, and the Revolution has yet to come.

Day 34

In my cell it is as dark as it is quiet. My days are filled with this solitude. The bird has yet to come back. I can hear footsteps once in a while, but no human or humane voices. Sometimes I hear echoes of the guards speaking to each other, but it never seems real. Once I heard someone walk up to my cell and look through the peephole—I know it was Mr. Soleymaani.

The attendant who gave me this pen has long been gone, replaced by one so gruff that I try to avoid any possible interaction. The first few times I said hello but he never replied. When he shoves the meal through the slot, I keep silent and still so as not to attract any undue attention. He manages to startle me at times, disrupting my normal routine.

Most of all, what I hear is the friction caused by my own body: my limbs rubbing against each other or the ground, my fingernails digging into my scalp, the air passing through my nostrils, or the forced expulsion of phlegm in the form of a cough. Sometimes, if I concentrate hard enough, I think I can hear the distant screams from the torture chamber, but I am never quite sure how much is my own invention.

And so it was when I heard the weeping for the past several nights. The weeping was so soft, like a great sorrow bound tightly inside, only once in a while releasing the slightest high-pitched sound, like a whimpering dog.

Again, I heard it two nights ago. By now I knew that it was the sound of a woman crying. I listened and listened in the dark and finally realized it was coming from the hole in which I relieve myself. The sound travels from the depths below, going upwards through the stench of acrid urine and foul feces stuck against the sides, upwards until it reaches the bars above and the sky beyond. I began imagining things about her. She must be new to be crying, she must be young and political. I pictured their secret meetings, plans for demonstrations. Then there was the inevitable infiltration and roundup.

After writing the last paragraph, Arash carefully folded the paper and tore the section out. He placed it in his mouth and began chewing on it as he thought of all of the events of the past day.

Yesterday while laying there, ear next to the hole, he had heard even more noises. He distinctly heard a cell door open and close. There was a shuffling of feet. Then he heard voices.

"Please, mister, I have a husband, I have a child, would you treat your—"

"Shut up!"

"Don't you have a mother or sister?" she pleaded, almost crying.

"I said shut up!"

There was the sound of a slap and a scuffle, then grunts and squeals. After the first few moments, Arash knew what was happening. He listened to it, not out of any pleasure, but rather a morbid curiosity.

The sounds were repeated today. He could not bear to hear it again, so he hummed a tune for half an hour before going back to the hole. What is to be done? he thought to himself. What can I tell her to make her forget—even if only for a few moments—the pain of a wound that will never completely heal? There is really no way I can relate, except in the walls that separate us and the filthy hole that connects us.

Day 35

> *I am beginning to hear sounds that should never have been made, noises that make me ashamed to be of this country. And yet I listen to them from beginning to end.*

There were many things on his mind but he knew he could not write about her directly.

That same night, while she was weeping, Arash whispered down the hole, "Miss! Miss!"

Arash put his ear to the hole and listened. She had stopped weeping.

"Listen, I am a prisoner too, your neighbor. I can hear you crying through the hole. My name is Arash. If you ever want to talk, just call up the hole."

He waited long for a reply, his ear straining for any noise, voice, or movement. Arash could no longer hear her crying. He knew she was forcing all the sounds inside, huddled in a far corner of the cell, crying bitter tears to herself. With these events now dominating his mind, Arash's plans to write about the Revolution were forgotten.

Day 36

During the past few days, all my worries have left me. What is a cough compared to all the other problems of this world? Sometimes I dream of the day when I will destroy this building. But I know it would not solve anything. It is the people and the way of thinking that needs to be changed. Without that, a new building would be erected for each one downed, just as a new Khomeini would rise from the ashes of the old.

* * *

There I was, lying on the cold ground, staring into the darkness, when I heard a voice, a whisper, soft and smooth, calling to me. It was a heavenly voice, a human voice.

"Mister, mister, can you hear me?"

Arash jumped up and scurried to the hole. Because of the stench, he had a habit of sleeping in the corner of the cell farthest away from the hole, so he was not sure if he had really heard anything. Arash put his ear to the hole. He held his breath as he strained to hear any sound, but no reply came.

"Miss, did you call me?"

"Yes," she whispered back.

They were both silent for what seemed like an eternity. Arash did not know what to say or how to proceed. What could he possibly say that actually meant anything? They had never seen each other. All he knew was that she had been raped. What did she know about him? How did she know he was not an informer?

"What is your name?" she finally asked.

"Arash, pleased to meet you. And what is your name?"

"Parvaneh."

"*Parvaneh*," he repeated, imagining a butterfly in his mind, "Parvaneh, if only you could grow wings and fly away."

"I have no windows here anyway."

"I have one, way above my head. I think we are in a tower."

"A window, how lucky you are."

"Right now I can see the moonlight. Once a bird came to my windowsill and sang for a while."

"You can see moonlight?"

"Yes."

"Can you please describe it for me?"

Arash took a moment to look at the light again and said, "The light is beautiful, white and silver. It leaves a shadow on the wall. I can see four strips of moonlight surrounded by blackness."

"That sounds beautiful. It is pitch-black in here. The only time any light comes in here is when they open the door."

They both became silent. She was in thought. He was embarrassed.

"Parvaneh?" Arash finally asked.

"Yes."

"How long have you been here?"

"I think close to a week."

"Have you been counting the meals?"

"Yes, twelve so far."

"And you came straight to isolation?"

"Yes."

"Then you've been here for twelve days. They only bring one meal a day, at least that's what they bring me."

"And how long have you been here?" she asked.

"I don't know anymore—months."

"What do they bring you to eat?"

"Bread and water. And you?" Arash asked.

"That's all? They give me *polow khoresh*, sometimes *ku ku*. I thought I wasn't getting enough food."

"At least I get the room with a view," Arash joked.

They were silent for a while before she asked, "But aren't you sick? I hear you coughing day and night."

"Yes."

"What's wrong with you, if you don't mind me asking?"

"I have TB."

"How do you know?"

"It's a long story," Arash replied.

"What about medicine, or have you seen the doctor here?"

"A doctor?" Arash said laughing. He laughed so hard that he started to cough. "A doctor? They've even stopped bringing my medicine."

"But why?"

"At first I thought it was more out of incompetence, then I thought that they were trying to kill me. Why else would they withhold my medicine and feed me only bread? For a while it confused me. But now I don't think any of it makes a difference or is even worth consideration. The situation is *khar tu khar,* and they kill each of us a different way."

Parvaneh became quiet and said goodnight shortly afterwards.

Day 37

Today I am afraid the door will open again.

Arash had been thinking about Parvaneh all day. He had been keeping away from the hole because he could not bear to hear the rape again.

Was there any way out of her predicament? Surely money given to the right people, but in these cells it was impossible to communicate with the outside. Maybe, he thought, she had family members already working to get her released.

Arash paced in his cell. Besides the two obvious choices, action and inaction, Arash could not think of any possibilities. He briefly flirted with the idea of using the hole similar to an intercom he heard from time to time. He quickly concluded this was a bad idea, and the more he thought about it, it seemed like a scene out of a bad movie.

Arash thought that this dilemma was not only Parvaneh's but also his own. How should one fight back? Before coming to prison, he had given this same question a lot of consideration. Should one fight back with action or non-action? What would you do, Mr. Ghandi? he now thought to himself. Would you let your wife be violated and your throat slit? Likely, the rapist would not stop on account of his conscience. In order for ahimsa to work, there needed to be a third party observer to exert pressure on the violator. Ghandi didn't have preconditions for non-violence, Arash thought, but what was the use of sitting idly while the knife penetrated the heart? If ahimsa was to better one's life, what use was it to lie dead in the corner of the cell? That would be the real violation, an innocent life lost without any repercussion. This was no time to test theories, he thought; the guard would rape her again, and no one would be there to care, not even Ghandi. If I had a gun, Arash thought, I'd shoot the lout myself: there's no other choice, she'll have to fight back.

"Arash, Arash, are you there?"

"Yes."

"I'm scared."

"Parvaneh, when I first came here I was scared too."

"What were you scared of?" she asked him.

"Death…and knowing I won't leave here."

"I'm not scared of death, Arash, I'm scared of the jailor."

There was silence. Arash knew this was her way of telling him.

"I've been thinking a lot. I don't know how to say this, but I think you need to fight back."

"But I've tried that already. He just hits back harder."

"You have to catch him off-guard. Show no resistance initially, don't shy away. Smile if you can manage it, walk up to him, undo his pants, and then do something extreme—squeeze his balls with all your might or bite his penis. You may get beaten up but he may not come back."

She did not answer him. She began to cry. Arash felt horrible. She did not need combat tactics, she needed human contact, someone to talk to, someone to hold. In America, he thought, they have people especially trained to talk about such issues. Who am I to coach her, what have any of my plans done for me?

"Parvaneh, Parvaneh, forget about all I said. I'm sorry I don't know how to help."

* * *

Arash was sleeping that night when he heard her voice. It was Jzaleh, she was staring into his eyes. She was saying, "Arash, Arash…"

Arash woke up to hear Parvaneh calling him, "Arash, Arash…"

"Yes."

"Sorry to wake you."

"It's alright."

"Who's Jzaleh? You kept calling that name when I called you."

"She was my girlfriend."

"You'll have to tell me about her later. Listen, I just woke up myself, it was the first time I slept soundly since I have been here. I thought about what you said and I did it! You don't know how hard it was to put on a fake smile when he came in and to actually go towards him, but I did it. When I gained his confidence, I squeezed them so hard he cried. Then I bit his arm. He could not even move for a few minutes. That's when I got scared. There was no where to run. He got up and beat me afterwards. I have a bloody nose and my eyes feel swollen, but he did not violate me."

At that moment Arash was so full of emotion that he could not reply.

"Arash? Can you hear me?"

"Yes, sorry. I'm so happy right now."

* * *

That night Parvaneh finally spoke about herself. She was a professor of sociology at the university, and not political at all. She was married and had two small children. One of her students had reported her. The student did not like a comment Parvaneh had made during a lecture dealing with the recent changes in Iran. She was taken at night from her house and brought straight to Evin. They had not interrogated her yet.

Arash told her a little about himself. But his cough was so severe that he could not complete half of his sentences. He told her about Jzaleh. She did not ask him how it was that he came to Evin and he did not volunteer the information. It is better if no one knows, he thought.

After a while, she became quiet and withdrawn, and Arash could no longer engage her in conversation. They said goodnight. Soon after, the sounds of weeping once again drifted into his cell.

Day 38

Every day, if I place my tray through the slot on the bottom of the door, I get a bowl of water and a piece of bread, a piece of sangak *bread. There is not much with which to amuse myself here and as this cell is utterly devoid of any color or pattern, anything at all which is visually pleasing (excepting the window), day after day I find myself looking at this bread. It is the only thing here that ever changes. It always has that creamy light yellow base, but the length and width vary so. My favorite is the end part, oval and usually a bit more meaty and much tastier, even when stale. The craters, too, capture my attention. They each have different sizes, and sometimes there is even a pebble or two that I have to pick out, setting them aside for closer examination later.*

Today I was staring at this bread and I wondered if they have a bakery here or if the bread is brought from outside Evin. I suppose it does not really matter, but how much of our days are filled with such nonsense? Then I began thinking of my sister. I do not know if it was the sangak *bread or the butterfly I saw in the window that made me think of her.*

There was a noonvai *right next to Naaser Agha's store which Naazi and I went to every day. I even went to visit the store a few months after I had come back to Tehran. The main purpose of the visit, though, was to see our old house. When I used to think about Pahlavi Street, how grand it seemed, a boulevard with two lanes on each side. But returning there after all these years, how it seemed to have shrunk! It was teeming with traffic that was pushing and pulling its way through the tiny lanes. From there I spotted the pharmacy, a landmark still intact, and made my way to our old house.*

But it was not an easy walk by any means. Although I still recognized the major landmarks such as the roundabouts and intersections, it all seemed to be from a different reality, seen through different eyes—and they were. When I was last in these parts, I was half as tall, and so it all seemed twice as big: the walls over which I could not see were no longer insurmountable, the ditch my foot would get stuck in was now just a large crack. There had been no gradual adjustment; I was not able to grow with the neighborhood. Now I wondered, was it really I who walked on these sidewalks? Was it really I who knew this place like the palm of my own hand, only to be a stranger to it now?

Once on our street, I found the house without much difficulty. To my dismay, they had painted the front door green instead of the brown that I was used to. The ivy that had covered all the walls around our house was now cleanly stripped. I walked further into the alley, in the back where we used to play football during the day and hide-and-seek at night. I walked towards the komiteh *and the spot where the* pasdar *had threatened me. There were no* pasdars *or even a guardhouse out front. Maybe the building was converted to something else, or maybe they ceased to be when there was no longer a threat of losing power.*

How different and empty it all seemed. Had we really lived our lives here? And where had they all gone, those people, those memories? I still remember the phone number to our house, 25-67-44; it is the only one I remember from all the places I have lived. Six numbers that have no meaning to anyone but me.

I hadn't the heart to ring the doorbell to our former house, but I told myself that if I spotted any people going into or out of the house, I would ask them, as a favor, to let an old inhabitant have a look around. It was early afternoon and they all must have been at school or work, as there was no one about. It was just as well, I was feeling somewhat sad and nostalgic already.

From there I walked toward Naaser Agha's store. His store was still in business, but there was no trace of the bustling noonvai *that used to be nearby. I walked up the stoop where my sister and I ate our snacks. I stood there a moment before going into the store.*

Naaser Agha was now an old man. Although he always seemed a lot older than us, seeing him like this was surprising to me. He appeared to be within the vicinity of his eightieth year, gray hair now white, wrinkles now deep furrows. He was reading the newspaper, as always. It was a copy of Hamshari. He put his newspaper aside and said, "Salaam."

"Salaam," I said, smiling, "One Pofak and one Kit Kat."

He replied, "I am sorry sir, I'm hard of hearing. Did you want Kit Kat or Tak Tak?"

I realized my mistake. I had said Kit Kat out of reflex, thinking about the old days. He went on, "Because, as you know, we haven't had Kit Kat for twenty years. It was an American company and you know how that goes. We have Tak Tak now," he said smiling, "our own invention, backwards like everything else, but in this one instance almost the same."

"So make that a Tak Tak instead," I said laughing.

I paid him and left. How happy I was as I sat on the stoop and ate my Pofak and Tak Tak, thinking of my sister. She had a sweet tooth and I a love for things salty. After finishing, we would get a drink from the communal tank in front of the store. It was cylindrical with four legs, silver-colored, with a metal cup chained to it, dangling by its side. It was placed next to the joob, and with one leg shorter than the others, it was leaning over and looked like it was about to fall. It was still there, as rusty and beaten-up as ever, with the same tilt. We always stopped there before going to the noonvai.

And what bread it was! The line was usually long, but we didn't mind waiting because it was always interesting to see them make it. There were always three or four workers inside. Behind the toil of these men, there was a warm flickering light coming from the oven, which baked the bread and made the workers sweat from morning till night. One man made the dough, mixing the flour with the right amount of water, kneading it thoroughly. Another placed a small mound of this dough evenly upon a flat, square board at the end of a long wooden pole. He would then place this deep within the mouth of the oven, which was filled with a mound of hot pebbles.

The square dough was placed at the top of this small hill, out *of view. As the dough was dragged down by gravity, it elongated slowly, narrowing a bit as it flowed down like lava, gathering fiery hot stones that became embedded in the solidifying dough, giving it deep, charred craters. When the bread was ready, it would be pulled out by the long pole. The bread would be slapped by a small broom to loosen the pebbles and then placed before us on a metal grill. We would pick off the remainder of the hot stones, which would fall on the floor, and go off with the bread, heading towards home.*

All the sad events of the day faded away as I thought of the little girl who was by my side, playing and joking all the way home. I thought of our mother, and how happy she would be when we brought the bread home, and how she would break off a piece and place it in her mouth while it was still hot.

All this business about going to Naaser Agha's was Naazi's idea in the first place. I had spoken to Naazi several times from Tehran, but it was always the superficial exchange that stems from using a public phone, the high cost of such calls, and the delay in transmission that effectively breaks up the momentum and natural flow of conversation.

I feel the last time I truly talked to her was before I left America, when she made me promise her that I would go to Naaser Agha's and buy a Kit Kat and sit on the stoop and think about the old days, when all three of us were still living together. This was near the end of our talk when she had finally accepted that I was leaving.

The last time I actually saw her was at our mother's funeral, when she came and stayed for a week in California. Once our mother died, it seemed as if the ties that were holding us together were severed in the same manner that my ties to America were to become.

I talked to Naazi a few times after that but our conversations were always strained, so that the intervals between phone calls grew longer and longer. In the past, when I had brought up going to Iran, she and my mother would gang up on me. When I was in high school, beyond the regular arguments, the one that hit me the hardest was, "You don't have enough money to go, you'll need 10,000 dollars to buy your exemption from conscription." This was true and so I gave up going for the time being.

When I was in college, my desire to return resurfaced and the 10,000 dollars, though a large sum of money, no longer seemed unobtainable. Then they would say, "First finish your schooling so you can make enough money to go." The real reasons lay elsewhere and we all knew this was only a delay tactic.

My college years were a mess. I tried to stay in school but my heart wasn't in it. It dragged on a few more years than it should have but I finally realized that it was not for me. Had I more ambition or attended a better school, I may have pursued Iranian Studies, as that was the only subject I was ever interested in. Instead, I moved in with my mother and started on a series of miserable jobs, one after another, for the sole goal of raising money. Once my mother caught wind of what was going on, she made it harder for me. First by charging rent and eventually persuading me to move out. She would tell me, "We came here by surmounting a thousand misfortunes and now you want to go back and sit next to a louse-ridden Akhound, *and for what?"*

I could never explain my feelings to her and she just could not understand. She was Iranian through and through. I thought her to be a tree with roots that were strong, firm, and immutable. I had been transplanted while still immature, with roots that were small and malleable, requiring constant nourishment and attention to prevent withering. And these dull roots ached with an intensity that made everything else seem insignificant.

"You've been here most of your life," she would say, "you're American." But that was not how I felt.

My mother then unexpectedly passed away. It took me some time to recover from that loss, and by the end of it I was convinced more than ever that my place was in Iran. There was not much of an inheritance with all of the debt and funeral expenses. I still did not have the total sum, but by then it hardly mattered.

So when I called Naazi, I knew she would not be pleased. When I told her my decision she reflexively went into the same mode, reciting the same tired arguments as our mother. "No, you don't understand!" I said emphatically, "I've bought my ticket, I have my passport. I'm going for good."

There was a great silence on the other end. Then she spoke in Persian, a language we no longer used when talking to each other. She pleaded, "Don't go, Don't go…"

Her voice was full of emotion and she began to cry. I knew she was crying for our mother and us, too, and me. As much as I loved my older sister, there was a part of me that always looked down on her. How could she have turned her back on us? How could my own sister want to forget about her past? She married an American, settled down far away from us (in Denver), and barely seemed to acknowledge her Iranian roots. I never considered how hard it must have been for her as well, nay how much harder as she tried to erase that part of her. How could she? How could anyone?

Now, as I await the end, I realize what a mistake I made. Instead of supporting her the way my mother did, my stance had only made us grow further apart. Gur-e pedar-e Irani budan, *having a sister is more important. I wish I could have done things differently.*

We stood on opposite battlefields, but that day we made peace with each other. Maybe it came too late, as I have not seen her since. But it was then, at the end of the conversation, after we had talked about ourselves, our mother, and my upcoming move, that she said, "You have to go to Naaser Agha's, buy Pofak *and Kit Kat, sit on the stoop, and think about the time when all three of us lived together. Promise me?"*

I wish I could see her one last time.

Parvaneh does not answer when he calls. He no longer hears her crying. He hopes she has been released, moved out of isolation, or at least at her trial, but he fears the worst has happened.

Day 39

Was it worth it, one or two nights of almost restful sleep? I cannot answer that.

There is a bit of selfishness, too. I am lonely once again, lonely in this tower.

Day 42

Still nothing.

So why did I come back? Life here has not been princely, or even akhondi *for that matter. For the answer to that we will need to talk to a man (with a striking resemblance to myself) standing on the corner of Jordan waiting for a ride. I can see him standing there, in a pitch of nervousness and anticipation. He is cleanly shaven and showered, his black hair cropped short, his clothes freshly ironed, without even a single wrinkle. His brown eyes try to appear calm as he glances at each passing car.*

Excuse me sir, could you tell me why have you come back?

That's a funny question, that's exactly what she asked.

She?

Yes, don't you remember Jzaleh?

Jzaleh?

Yes, I was standing on the corner of Jordan waiting for a ride. This was the second time I stood there, and this time it was no accident. How long had it been since I last had female contact? Sure, there was the occasional brushing up against breasts while walking through a door, or the extra pressure of a sumptuous body when the bus swayed to one side, though one had to make sure one obtained a spot in the back or there was no hope for action. But these tactics, even when successful, only led to more frustration. I had seen men groping women on crowded buses, when the sheer numbers ensured that no clean line could separate the men in the front from the women in the back. Usually there would be a scream, a slap, or a loud complaint, but once in a while the recipient did not seem to mind.

I had become quite adept at reading into the monteau's *curves, imagining what pleasures lay beneath. In the West, little imagination is needed, but here, the face and eyes take on tremendous importance, as does the cut of a* monteau. *The* chador *reveals nothing about the body and rather too much of the dogmatic mind, but there is something to behold in the finer cut of a* monteau. *The curves, so carefully covered, still trigger a primal need that can not be denied. Add a bit of a strut and a dash of perfume, the glimpse of an ankle or wrist, and that is enough to drive any man crazy.*

But where to meet these women? I was cut off from the usual avenues such as family, friends, and work. Furthermore, even had I met someone, we could not go out on a date or even walk together in public. I knew there had to have been an outlet besides what I had already seen. Besides, I did not want to become a molester. Once I learned the true meaning of "San Francisco," the world seemed to smile upon me again. All my other activities were suspended as I headed straight for Jordan and joined the other young men waiting to get picked up. I had shaved and showered. I wore jeans and a clean, designer, long-sleeved shirt. It was not long before the cars began to slow down, with each of the female drivers surveying me from head to toe. One stopped in front of me. The driver smiled. I hurriedly got in. Before I even said hello, she stepped on the accelerator.

"Salaam, my name is Jzaleh" she said without a hint of unease, "what's your name?"

"Arash."

We were both silent for a few moments. She was wearing her floral patterned rusari *rather loosely, and I could see a good portion of her wavy black hair. She was pretty and well-off, I could see that right away, but at that moment I was more worried about getting caught. I kept leaning forward to check the side mirror for any cars that might be following us.*

She gave a quick look at me and said, "Don't worry, I've got plenty of money in case we get pulled over. This must be your first time, no?"

"Sort of, let's just say the last time I got in a bit of trouble."

"OOO—a basiji *story. You have to tell me," she said smiling.*

"It was quite by accident, really—"

"Let me guess, you were trying to flag down a taxi when a lady stopped and you got in—"

"Exactly, how did you know?" I asked with surprise.

"Don't look so shocked, tell me the real story."

"That is the real story."

"So you mean to tell me—"

She stopped mid-sentence and pulled over, braking rather abruptly. She frowned and looked at me curiously before saying, "Where are you from anyway?"

"Do you think I have an accent?"

"Not until now, but yes you have a small one."

"You really think so? I have been trying to get rid of it. I used to live in America."

She gave a quick look to her left before pulling back onto the main road. She was smiling while looking ahead. She then gave a few glances in my direction and very seriously said, "America is it? So you left us when it got too hot, so you didn't have to fight. You've lived your life of luxury over there and now you're back?"

I could not figure out whether she was joking or not. Regardless, I was taken aback by the whole experience thus far. I had come for sex only and was not expecting such a forceful woman. I fell silent, not knowing what to say.

Then she smiled and said, "Hey, I was only joking you know, lighten up! Don't you know we're all jealous. Any one of us would kill to get out of here. Now tell me the rest of the story. I have a feeling it is not going to turn out well. So you really didn't know what you were doing?"

"No, I thought it very strange that she should pick me up but, of course, I didn't mind. I asked her where she was going, and she just laughed and said, 'San-Fran-cis-co.'"

Jzaleh, herself, now burst out laughing, saying, "You're lying! She did not say that!"

I nodded my head.

"And you didn't know what it meant?" she asked.

"It seemed strange to me, but I was so caught up in the moment, and then I thought if there could be a street name like

the Americas, then maybe there was a place by the name of San Francisco. I didn't ask because I didn't want to appear naive."

"But you know now?"

"Yes, but not before I accidentally came across Dai Jan Napelon *and read it."*

"You've never seen the television series, then…"

"I have a vague recollection of it from my childhood, nothing more. And I saw one or two episodes a few years ago, but that was all. Anyway, pretty soon we were pulled over. She told them I was her cousin. They asked for the papers, and she slipped in 2,000 tomans*—"*

"That's not enough!" Jzaleh exclaimed in surprise.

"Apparently not; they slapped her. Then I got out of the car, all worked up, yelling at the basiji, *when another jeep pulled up, and out came a whole gang of them. They started beating me up and she left in the confusion. They took me to Valsadr, I think it's called, where I stayed overnight. The next day at the hearing, after asking all the introductory questions, they asked where I was going with the lady. I was completely honest with him. I said I was just trying to get back to the hotel, but she wanted to go to a place called San Francisco."*

"Some in the room were chuckling, but the judge looked at me real angry and said, 'Who do you think I am?' He would not hear anymore. He slapped the heftiest fine on me and let me go."

By now Jzaleh was laughing hysterically. "That is the best story I have heard in a long time."

"It wasn't funny when it was happening."

"But now?"

I looked at her and said, "San-Fran-cis-co!"

We both laughed.

We drove through the streets of Tehran. That part of the city was full of stores with bright neon signs advertising luxurious goods. There were people walking on the sidewalks and in the parks. Once off the main roads, the streets were quieter, an odd person walking or a car going the opposite way. Soon she pulled in front of a gate. She got out and opened it and then drove the car onto the driveway.

Once inside, I saw that the driveway was at the southern most section of the property. There was a gentle slope northwards with a garden leading the way to the house. The grass was trimmed neatly and the trees were symmetrically spaced throughout the garden. Rose bushes lined the eastern and western walls all the way up to the house. There was a gravel path through the garden, leading to the house. We walked along it.

"This is incredible," I said.

"Thank you. This is my parents house."

"You don't live here?"

"Yes, but we also have an apartment in Shahrak-e Gharb, which I pretty much have for myself. My parents are liberal that way. Anyway, they're away this weekend."

We came upon a bench. She said, "Let's sit here for a bit."

She lifted her veil, officially inviting me into a forbidden world. Although it was dark, there was enough ambient light for me to see her. Thick black, wavy hair hung to below her shoulders. A smile came across her well-formed lips, as her dark brown eyes peered into my own. Her eyebrows had been meticulously trimmed, like smooth blades of grass. Her already dark eyelashes were colored black, pointing slightly outwards.

From where we sat, a large weeping willow was in view, its long branches, like tentacles, gently swaying in the breeze. The moon was shimmering through its leaves and above the tree I saw the stars. I was nervous. I reached out for her hand, so soft and warm as it rubbed against my own that I could not believe the sensation I was feeling. I had not had any physical contact for such a long time that I felt I was a teenager again, having my hand held for the first time. Soon we were kissing and before long we went inside and made love.

As we lay there in the dark, I was feeling awkward as I had never before been intimate with someone I knew so little. On top of it all, I was a bit embarrassed at having performed so poorly, being so out of practice and at such a pitch of excitement. We were both looking at the ceiling. She was the first to break the silence.

"Tell me about where you've lived all this time."

"I was born in Tehran—"

"I mean abroad."

"We left here in 1983, let's see…that's 1362 over here—"

"Who's 'we'?"

"Me, my mother, and my sister. My father died when I was very young—I don't remember him at all. I think he had a problem with his liver or kidney. Anyway, we left in the middle of the war."

"How did you get out—through Turkey?"

"No, nothing that dramatic. I knew someone, though, who went out that way, with the shepherds, sheepskin on their back, moving with the herd as the helicopters patrolled overhead. What a story that was—they barely made it, passed on from tribe to tribe, some decent and some opportunistic. Once they were even stripped of everything but their clothes, left to die in the cold.

We left legally, by airplane, with visas to Spain, then England. I was so happy to leave. By then I had had enough. Also, even though I was the only male, there was the threat of the draft.

You should have seen me those first few days in Madrid. We had come from Tehran in the midst of war to a peaceful Western nation. Where were you during the war?"

"I was in Tehran the whole time," she said, "eight long years… Remember how they told us that if we were outside during a bombing to seek shelter in the joob *because it was below ground level?"*

Now recalling her childhood memories, she sat up in bed and continued, "Remember how every night the radio would give off the emergency siren, all the power to the city would be cut off? We would go to the basement. We still had to do our homework, so we did it by candlelight."

"Yes," I said, "we had to study by candlelight also. I could

never concentrate on my homework because I would play with the fire and hot wax. Once, I even almost burned our house down. I had put the candle on the ground to tie my shoelaces but the candle fell over, lighting a tablecloth. I ran to the bathroom and brought back a bucket of water and put out the fire. I got into a lot of trouble because everyone knew I played with fire and so the accident story was hard to believe.

A few times, after we got used to the nightly bombings, I would go to the window. Once I saw the Iraqi airplanes as they went by, with the trail of anti-aircraft fire following, but our neighborhood was never bombed."

"We weren't so lucky," she said, "a bomb landed a few blocks away. It was so loud that I couldn't hear a thing for a few days. It shook our entire house, breaking all the glass. There was smoke all around. I thought we were all going to die that night."

We were both silent for a while before I broke in with, "It's strange isn't it? When I lived here, everything that happened to me seemed to be the normal state of things. If I got bullied in school for not being poor, or if we had to study by candlelight because of the bombing raids, those became the daily facts of life, although even then I could have told you something was wrong. So now picture going from the situation here to a city where there was law and order. Where the cars stopped at red lights, where the streets were clean, where milk was easily obtained at any store, where you felt safe."

She turned to me and asked, "How long were you in Europe?"

"We were in Madrid and London for only a few months before we went to America."

"So Europe and America is just like they say it is. But why did you come back?"

"It sounds nice doesn't it? America. The world dreams of America. The main advantage of America is that on paper everyone is equal, at least everyone who is a citizen. I am grateful they let us in and allowed us to live there. But America is not

what people here think it is. The images you get from the satellite dishes—that is Hollywood, the make-believe world of television where everybody has everything and is happy. There is some truth to it, maybe. But if you actually went to Hollywood you would see a different picture. But I do think the homeless person there is doing much better than the one here.

Our problems were different. First, we were immigrants, refugees. Our status was better than some of the others because we had money. But outside of the big cities, people would still look at you sideways if you had an accent. On top of that we were associated with Moslem fundamentalism and terrorism; they still remembered the hostages and resented us for it. God forbid if you had an Arab sounding name like Mohammad, Ali, or Hossein. I can't tell you how many times I was stopped at the border or airports because of my last name, my birthplace, or the way I looked—dark skin and eyes, thick hair and eyebrows. Many times the racism was so subtle that I didn't notice it when I was younger, but years later I would recall an event and it would make sense. Even so, it was still less of a hassle to live over there compared to the everyday stupidity experienced here. But that is not all.

Do you know how many people hid the fact that they were Iranian? If asked where they were from, they would somehow evade the question, or if pressed, their reply would be Italy or even Persia. Persia, that fabled land, romantic sounding to Western ears, that very few knew was in reality our own Iran. I knew that feeling of shame all too well, when the look on the other person's face would change and they would say, "Oh." I called myself Persian, too, when I first went over there, when I learned the word Iranian held such negative connotations. It was such a shock when I learned that the Iran that was part of me was considered evil. I only did it two or three times, but each time I would get such a horrible feeling that I no longer could do it.

After that first phase I would tell them I was from Iran, but then try to explain to them that Iran was more than what they saw on TV, which was the hostages, Khoemini, and terrorism. It was hard to battle the media and always be on the defensive. In the end I no longer cared, no longer gave an explanation after I told them I was from Iran. If someone was curious, I would tell them about Iran. Otherwise, I kept the matter to myself. In this way I think I slowly drifted away from assimilation and into my own.

I was younger then—you know I studied engineering for no other reason than I was good at math. Is that any way to make a life's decision? Anyway, I never finished college. Something within me gave out. I worked jobs here and there, but my only true passion was Iran.

At the same time, each day I was living there I felt less Iranian, I couldn't help it. Maybe it was easier for the older folks to adjust there since they were already so firmly rooted in Iran. I was not turning my back on my culture like my sister did. On the contrary, I would read my Iranian books, listen to Iranian radio, eat my chelo kabob, *go to the Iranian parties. But there was something missing.*

I think the Iranians who moved to California had a lot of money and so it always seemed everyone was concerned about status. The parties seemed so shallow and fake, the only concern was who had more money or a better car, or whose child went to a more prestigious college. Maybe I never found the right crowd. I would still go to the parties but I never felt comfortable there. It bore very little relation to the Iran I knew.

At night I would think about Iran. In my homesickness I would picture Tehran like it was before the Revolution: the tree-lined boulevards, the magnificent backdrop of Damavand, even the sad call of the muezzin as it echoed in the streets and alleys—"

"Don't tell me you had romantic notions of the Akhounds!*"*

"No, me of all people! Those bastards can go to hell, but the local mullah, I don't think, can be all that bad or else he would be hiding in his mansion. His cry always touched me, like one pleading to God. Anyway, like it or not they are part of who we are."

I looked at her and smiled, "Yes, I admit it! In a way, I even missed the goddamn mullahs—but don't tell anyone."

We both laughed.

"I could see all the events that had happened unfold before my eyes. My grandparents' house, the cheap plastic balloon of a ball we learned to play football with in the alleys. I was twelve the first time I saw a real football field with grass. I couldn't believe my eyes. We ran onto the field yelling and screaming, jumping and tumbling on the grass. When the action was on the other side of the field, I would look across the adjacent fields. The green carpet spread out like a big meadow with the sun slowly reaching the horizon. Kneeling on the ground, I ran my hands through the blades of grass which felt like silk to me.

Even in the bad experiences, there was a richness not present in my memories from the West. How many football fields I would see in America and how many perfect things, but in all those memories there is a hue of loneliness and isolation. The line of separation in my memories is that fateful day I left Iran, as if the events in my mind changed abruptly from color to black and white."

We lay naked in the dark for a while and my thoughts drifted to the present. It was strange, I thought, beginning a relationship in this manner. We did not really know each other, yet the ultimate act of intimacy had taken place.

She spoke now. "I always imagined life over there would be great. The clothes, stores, freedom. We always thought that you were the lucky ones, the winners. I never knew there was such a cost."

"I think the immigration took its toll on everybody, whether you found a way to live with it or not—I have to tell the story of Feerooz sometime. Anyway, my mother, who loved Iran and whose thoughts were always here, vowed never to come back unless the regime changed. She once told me she did not want her memory of the Iran she knew to be altered by the current reality, it would be too upsetting for her. I had been wanting to come here for

years, but she was completely against it. I was younger, too, and didn't think I could come here without her contacts, friends in Tehran or relatives in Isfahan. Once she died, there was nothing holding me back."

"So both your parents are dead?"

"Yes."

"I'm sorry to hear that. I imagine that must be hard."

"Yes and she was the only family I had."

"So you were an only child?"

"I have a sister, but she's married and lived far away from us. Anyway, we've grown apart. I have other family, but they're scattered all over Europe and America. So it wasn't a hard decision for me to come here."

"And you have some family here, in Isfahan, you said?"

"Yes, but I can't say I really know them. They're my mom's cousins. I only saw them a few times as a child and not at all in the last fifteen years... So tell me about your family."

"My father is a businessman, doing quite well as you can see. My mother is a housewife. I don't have any brothers or sisters."

"And what about you?"

"I went to university and got a degree in chemistry. But I haven't been able to get a job since I finished four years ago."

"Why not?"

"Because of the economy and the fact that I am a woman. I've had one or two offers but I got the feeling they wanted to hire me for something else."

"Really? So what have you been doing?"

"Dodging the suitors my parents throw at me," she said with a chuckle.

"That's a horrible situation to be in."

"You're telling me," she said.

We were both silent for a few moments before I asked, "Don't you think our encounter is a bit strange?"

"Yes," she said laughing, "who would have thought I picked up an American!"

"No, I mean how everything is backwards. The sex first, then the getting to know each other."

"You will get used to it, everything is backwards here. Sometimes this is the only way we can meet someone. Once in a while you might meet someone at a party. But this doesn't feel strange to me. I've had one boyfriend I met this way. Sometimes it's just one night. I thought in America sex was pretty open."

"It can be, but I don't think most people go about it like this. I mean, here, sometimes in the stores schoolgirls will brush against me."

She rolled on top of me and whispered in my ear, "Like this?"

* * *

Jzaleh and I continued to see each other. We bought a forged document stating I was her cousin, and in this way we were able to go out in public without fear. We went to the movies, restaurants, and on weekends we hiked in the mountains, just a bit north of where I am now.

On the weekends it was a busy destination, filled with families and couples like us. Near the bottom it was more like a road than a hiking trail. Once you climbed past a few stations, the crowds thinned out. The air up there felt clean and crisp, and everybody was more relaxed as the basijis *did not usually venture that far up. With each meter of elevation, the scarves would move back a few millimeters, and off the trail, they would sometimes come completely off.*

Jzaleh would take me to her spot. It was off the trail, on a large rock overlooking Tehran. We would climb the rock and sit on top its relatively flat surface. Behind us was the rising mountain. There were no trees up there, only a few scrub brushes. And the only animal I ever spotted was the occasional small bird. The main view was that of Tehran below.

Once, while sitting there and looking at the view, I asked her, "What do you want out of life?"

She was silent a while and kept looking ahead.

"Look below," she finally said, "look at how beautiful it is. All those people living their lives in a city that was built in the middle of nowhere. I suppose I like the present, making the best of it."

Teasing her I said, "But you know the view is only good once a week."

"Maybe that's good enough—I don't know—sure, I wish things were better here. I would like to travel and see the world, eventually settle down and have a family, though not necessarily here."

"What about Iran?"

"What about it? We can't control what happens. And I can't worry about it all the time. My life would pass me by, even more than it has already. But I wish it was different and some days I more than wish it…"

She introduced me to many of her friends and I attended their parties. At first they were new and exciting for me. I felt like I had found the group I had been looking for. Looking back at them now, were they really any different than the ones in LA*? In America, the parties are an escape from the everyday culture of America, an opportunity to reaffirm one's own Iranian culture. In Iran, they are an escape from the Islamic culture of the* Akhounds*, effectively doing exactly the same.*

Sassan was right, we needed to be numb. And it was at the parties that people could vent their dissatisfaction with their jobs, the government, and the economy. The rusaris *came off and sexy evening wear took their place. Bootlegged* CDs *of Iranian and American pop music would be played. And alcohol—wine, beer, vodka—was the means of escape. Sometimes there would be opium but I was not there long enough to be invited.*

I took refuge in Jzaleh as she did in me. We gave each other the companionship we needed and no longer felt alone. She now had someone beside her at these gatherings, and I now had a social life. But we had a much better time alone, when it was just the two of us.

The last party I went to was at Jzaleh's apartment. Her apartment had two bedrooms, a small kitchen, and a living room with a couch and several stand-alone chairs. I had arrived early to help her with the preparations. She was making salad olovieh *and cutlets for the guests. I tidied up the living room while she was in the kitchen. She called out to me, "I'm almost finished here, how about you?"*

"This room was already clean."

"Come here and taste the cutlet."

I went into the kitchen and she placed a small piece in my mouth.

"Very tasty."

She was chewing on a piece also and said, "I think it needs a bit more salt."

She took the salt shaker and sprinkled the batter with more salt. She looked over to me and said, "So have you thought about getting an apartment? It's not easy you know, you have to search, ask around, and sometimes they want exorbitant fees up front."

"I don't have much money."

"Come on, you have been staying in hotels all these months, which is more expensive? Another thing, aren't you tired of waking up in a hotel every day? I for one would go crazy," she said as she began to mold the cutlets and place them in the frying pan.

The truth was that my money really was running out. I had moved out of the Hotel Evin a long time ago and was gradually drifting south as the money got tighter, each time moving to a cheaper hotel of less quality. I was now staying at the Hafez Hotel but was considering a move to the Hotel Shams near the bazaar. I felt uncomfortable telling her, as I knew she would try to help me with money again.

The doorbell rang just then and soon the guests filled the tiny apartment. Some of the men had brought vodka and beer.

There were a handful of married couples, as well as single men and women. I knew Behrooz from before so I sat next to him. We both began to drink beers. Unlike some of Jzaleh's friends who were regulars at each and every gathering, Behrooz only came to a few. He had made a good impression on me as he was loud and energetic, and very political. I had a feeling he knew many people and was probably active in some political organizations.

"So how are things Behrooz?" I asked him.

"Nothing new, I've been working a lot at the office. We have a deadline that's coming up on one of our projects."

Behrooz turned to a man sitting next to him and asked, "When are you going to Canada?"

"We don't have our visa yet, but the embassy said it should be approved soon."

I turned to him and asked, "Can I ask why you're leaving?"

"I can't work in this environment any longer. Either you're comfortable with the hypocrisy or you're not. My coworkers, for example: there are a few of them who drink their alcohol like me, but we have to pretend all the time: pretend we don't drink, pretend we like the regime, pretend we like our jobs, all out of the fear of losing our lousy jobs. And the money isn't that good either. Right now I have to work two jobs just to make ends meet, that's with both of us working. Pretty soon you end up taking bribes without a moment's hesitation, and then what have you become?"

Another person chimed in, "All the while the government and its cronies are robbing us blind. There is this product X, mined from Iran. It is shipped to UAE, untouched, unrefined. They place a stamp on it, Made in UAE. They sell it to France for three times the money they bought it from Iran. France in turn sells it back to us, four times the price it was bought from UAE. The director in charge of purchases gets a percentage of all the sales, so instead of buying it from ourselves, he buys the inflated price."

One of the women spoke up, "Then there is Bonyad-e

Mostazafin. *Once accepted to the club, they're given a car, a large sum of money, and government loans. They even get this nice package if they move to a different department within the organization. So the first thing anyone does or the only thing they all do is submit for a transfer, push some paper for a month, then collect the new bonus."*

Another said, "Have you heard the entomologist's latest saying?"

He turned to me while laughing and said, "There is one politician from Ahvaz that the liberal newspapers call the entomologist, because he said he knew insects well, and that the followers of the current president were all insects! When asked to comment on the ozone layer he said, 'I don't know what is all this fuss over the ozone layer. I don't know much about the hole. I hear it is in Germany and Turkey. Let's keep it there. Let us knit it, sew it up, pour cement on it and then see what relevance it has to the Islamic Republic.' Can you believe that?! This illiterate idiot is a representative of the people, making critical decisions about our country every day, on topics he does not even understand. Imagine those under him!"

I turned to Behrooz, "What about the reformist movement, the student demonstrations?"

"I'm not sure they'll get anywhere. They came down on us so hard. Anyway, once they leave the university, most people start worrying about making ends meet, not politics."

The food was brought and then there was dancing. First to Iranian music, then in my honor, they played Michael Jackson. I did not have the heart to tell them that his excesses, personally and musically, represented the worst of American culture. They would not understand. As far as they were concerned, Michael Jackson was a symbol of America, and as I was from America, the two had to mix. I danced anyway. They were curious to see the Western style. Everyone was having fun. We drank more and more.

At one point Behrooz grabbed me by the shoulder and asked, "Tell me, what have you been doing with your time?"

"Most days I go around exploring Tehran, the different neighborhoods, shops, museums."

He started to laugh, "What a waste of time—and what have you found?"

"What do you mean?" I said, offended.

We were both drunk by now. He looked at me sarcastically, pointed at me and said, "Well, what great truths have you found?"

How could I answer him? The only truth that I knew was the feeling of loss that comes from leaving one's homeland. My time was spent in trying to reconnect with a life that had gone by.

"I don't know about any truths. I have been gone for fifteen years, and so much has happened in that time."

"Nothing good, only problems."

"Yes, a lot of problems."

"And what are they to you?" he quipped back.

I was taken aback and said, "What do you mean? I am Iranian—I want to see if anything can be done, to help."

"Help! Help!" cried Behrooz with his arms in the air, sarcastically laughing all the while. Then he stopped and looked more serious.

"There is no one to help us. What do you know about us anyway? You left and now you're back. You didn't have to serve time in the army like us. You don't have a job, you don't work with us, you don't have a house, you live in a hotel, you don't live with us. And tomorrow or the day after tomorrow you'll get on your plane and leave this hellish nightmare and forget about all of this. So now, how do you propose to help us?"

I had wanted Behrooz to introduce me to some of the student groups or other political organizations. I had wanted to tell him about my ideas, but with my hopes dashed, my only reply was, "I don't know."

Behrooz now stood up, with his beer in his hand. He spread his arms wide and said, "Everybody listen up! This American boy wants to help us in our lives. He has come here and single-hand-

edly will turn everything around. Now, does anyone have any requests?"

*The room was filled with laughter, everyone had their eyes on me. I felt humiliated. Someone shouted, "*Ahre Baba*! Your American passport, hurry up and pass it over here!"*

There was more laughter. Jzaleh, who was in the kitchen, came out smiling and asked, "What's going on, what's all the ruckus?"

Behrooz walked up to Jzaleh and took her arm, steering her over to me. He said, "We were just having a bit of fun Jzaleh Khanoom. *You have a good boy here; now where is that vodka?"*

I left soon afterwards.

* * *

His words tore into me. I walked away that night depressed. Everything he had said was true to a degree, but it did not sit right. I began to reevaluate my situation. Presumably, I had come back to live here but had done nothing towards that. I was not working. Nor did I really fit into any group I had met. And to those who knew my situation, I was merely a curiosity.

Behrooz was right, the regime affected me less than those around me. But the damage to me was done before, years ago, not only by what was done while I was in Iran but also by what had happened when they made us refugees, thus changing our lives forever. Now I had the shield of money which meant I did not have to work. Also, I was a man, a member of the lucky 50% that did not have to wear a veil every day, a tu-sari *as a reminder of the oppression. But the longer I stayed, the more uncomfortable I became as I saw the lives around me. Every time I saw a* basiji *beating up a teenage boy, I thought of the* pasdars *of our time. Every time someone complained of the hardships of daily living, I remembered our own.*

I had changed, too. The superficial ways, the accent and mannerisms, would eventually come back. But having tasted freedom and knowing there was a better way—that they could not take away. It is precisely for this reason that the Akhounds *could never fully implement the* hejab*: women knew what it was like to be* hejab*-less before the Revolution.*

One thing I knew was that no matter how bad my situation would become, no matter how bad the government was, I had come to stay. My fate, regardless of what Behrooz thought, was now tied with my countrymen. I would never leave, never go back to America.

I did not want to live the rest of my life in exile, dreaming of the past. Nor was I simply content to accept the present reality. I wanted to work for the future of Iran, to fulfill the promise of the past two revolutions, to have a government that was representative of the people. I knew and felt these things in America, but I was too far away then, too detached to give these thoughts much importance. Sure, like many exiles I wanted change but that was not all I lived for. I gave much more thought to the Iran I knew than to the future of the country. Even so, when I came back there was a small part of me that had come for that very purpose. Maybe that is why my family was so opposed to my going. Though I did not notice it at first, my desire to bring about change was growing day by day, and soon, the vague notion became a singular aim.

I stood by the side of road waiting for a cab. I looked up at the banner that went from one side of the street to the other. I didn't even bother reading it. I don't know why, but more than any other form of propaganda, these banners irritated me the most. I closed my eyes and imagined the banner engulfed in flames. I opened my eyes. It was still there. I don't even have a lighter, I thought. The headlights of an approaching cab caught my eye and I flagged it down.

It was late at night, and even though I was running out of money, I decided to go darbast. *The driver and I were both silent at first. I sat in the back seat but we were able to see each other through the rear-view mirror. He had black curly hair and was wearing glasses. I thought he was around forty years old. He opened up the conversation with small talk. He had an accent so I asked him where he was from.*

"Outside Shiraz."

I followed up with, "How long have you been in Tehran?"

"Most of my life."

"Are you married?"

"With two children, four and five years old. It's nice to have a big family, but I can barely afford it. I have a day job that pays 35,000 tomans *a month, then I drive the taxi until midnight or one."*

"So you don't see your family much?"

"Not as much as I'd like."

"They haven't had chicken in months. Things are so bad, the economy, that I haven't been able to buy meat."

"Still," he continued, "I don't regret having the children, they're all the family I have now. My mother died a few months ago."

"Khoda beyamorzadesh."

He became silent, perhaps again feeling the grief.

"What did she pass away from?"

"Nerves. It all happened after she found out my brother became a shaheed. *We found out a few years ago, in '74, almost 15 years after the fact. First they said he was a POW, then years later they told us he was dead. We never saw him, they just gave us a handful of bones."*

"How did you know it was him?" I asked.

"They sent us his glasses, his book, and wallet before sending him; all these things we recognized, but we wondered where his windbreaker was. When they sent him, it was with him. They had wrapped up his bones and body parts in his jacket."

"Did you bury him in Behesht-e Zahra?"

"No, we requested he be buried in the cemetery in the city

he was born. Ever since then she wasn't the same. Also, when I was in the Iraqi War they told her I had been captured, which wasn't true."

"How old are you?" I asked.

"Thirty-eight."

We were quiet again. I mustered enough courage to ask him what I thought was an even more intruding question than how his mother died.

"Do you have nightmares?"

"I still have them sometimes," he answered without surprise. He paused a moment before continuing, "When I think about the group of guys I was with, those killed, blown up, or the one who was paralyzed, I do think about them. One boy, after he was discharged, he came to see us. We told him not to come, to go straight home, but he didn't listen. See, any one of us would've done the same thing he did, we were family. That could have been any one of us. The jeep that he rode on was hit by a mortar shell. He was killed instantly. I had to carry him myself. It's a terrible thing, war…"

He shook his head in disgust.

"They show these movies on TV, it's not like that at all. We were hungry and thirsty, once we had to eat wild grass for four days. And water—there was a little spring, we had to strike it with our bayonets to get out water drop by drop as they shot at us. We even drank swamp water—green and smelly. Sometimes we couldn't take a shower for thirty days, so dirty."

He was shaking his head again. I asked him, "Did you ever fight face-to-face with the Iraqis?"

"Yes, I was almost captured once. I can tell stories, but you'll never know what it was like unless you've been there. Once there were fifteen of us in a hole when we were shelled on. We all clung to each other and half of us were killed."

There was silence now. He drove for a few blocks in his own reverie. He looked at me with a sad smile through the rear-view mirror and said, "I'll never forget this, about ten years ago I won the lottery for the Japanese work visa. It was a chance of a lifetime. I sold everything I had. Once I got it all together I had 100,000 tomans, *but I couldn't go. You needed 300,000* tomans *to go. I went and asked my father for the money but he couldn't get it. I tried and I tried—there was no way I could get it.*

I didn't go. I will never forget it, never. I still have my passport and visa, new as the day they gave it to me, but expired. Every time I think about it I get mad. Those who went there are doing well with cars and houses, and look at us—working like dogs—barely surviving."

"Does the government give you any money?" I asked.

"What? No!"

"Only those injured."

"Yes, only those. They can get all kinds of jobs."

Soon we were at the hotel. I gave him a little extra so he could buy meat for his children. He thanked me and wrote his number down on a piece of paper, in case I needed a taxi again. But those were the end of my darbast *days, and I never had an occasion to call on him.*

The next day I decided to go to the cemetery where my father was buried. I bought a few flowers and took a bottle of water with me. Though he was spoken of by my mother and my relatives many times, I never knew the man. He always seemed to be a distant relative, one I had heard stories about but had no real connection to.

The graveyard, though, I did remember. My mother used to go there weekly and we would accompany her once a month or so. It was an old place, with the main courtyard housing most of the graves. The tombstones were all rectangular, of all different sizes, embedded horizontally into the ground like pieces of a mosaic. One had to walk over them to get to the desired place. There were also private rooms on the sides of the courtyard, guarded by lock and protected from the elements. Many years ago the family had bought a large portion of it, so my father's parents were buried there and so on and so forth.

The entrance was off a busy street. The day I went to visit, there were throngs of schoolchildren standing outside the main entrance, to the side of the two large wooden doors leading to the courtyard. They seemed unnaturally quiet and ill at ease. One of their classmates had been struck and killed by a car. From inside I heard the howls of the mother. When I walked inside I saw her surrounded by family. She was wearing a black chador *and tears were streaming down her face. She was throwing her arms up in the air and screaming, "Oh God! My son, my unfortunate son! Oh God! Why him? Why my child? Oh God! What am I to do now?! Take me! Take me instead of him!"*

Everyone was looking at her sympathetically. But no one knows a mother's loss. She was soon escorted out by her family and a sense of calm returned to the graveyard. I walked across the courtyard to the area I knew my father's grave to be in. My grandparents were buried in one of the private rooms, but his grave was out in the open. I crouched down and tried to read the tombstones. With all the foot traffic and the accumulation of dirt, they were hard to read, as hard to read as some of the etchings on the walls of my cell. On a sunny day, I am able to make out the crude inscriptions on these walls, the tally of days and of poetry and long forgotten names. In the graveyard, water serves as the illuminator.

I poured the water over several tombstones. Suddenly the marble came to life, the dull and dirty white becoming creamy and sharp, the cryptic symbols now readable as the intricacy of the chiseled marble was revealed. I found his without trouble and poured more water, getting on my knees, using my hands to wash the marble. I read my father's name and that of his father. There was also written his dates of birth and death and a line of poetry. That is all that is left of him now, as the marks in this cell are all that is left of some of the former inmates. Maybe I should have felt something at his grave, but how could I have feelings toward someone I have no memories of?

How sad the graveyard always seemed to me. Naazi and I never liked going as our mother would cry each and every time we went there. But that is why I went back, for remembrance of my mother and not my father. I have so many memories of visiting the graveyard with my mother. How it pained her that we never got to know him. My mother would always try to bring him into our lives. Whenever there was a big decision to be made, to our chagrin, she would say, "Your father would have…"

And how much it pained her that we never willingly wanted to go to his grave. After all such visits, as a reward, she would take us out for ice cream. As we walked into the store, we would be greeted by the smell of rosewater, and soon we would be eating the rosewater ice cream placed between two crispy wafers. By then her spirits were usually better and we would have a good time. Still, when the time for the next visit came, Naazi and I were hesitant once again, looking for an excuse not to go.

I placed the flowers on his grave and walked over to my grandparents' graves. I was there for a few minutes before leaving.

* * *

By the next weekend I had come to a decision. I would move into the Hotel Shams and I would break up with Jzaleh. The first part was done easily enough, the second I knew would be much harder.

There was really nothing wrong with Jzaleh. I had seen some of the other women at the parties in Tehran, socialites whose only concern was the latest European and American fashions. And, in America, I had seen the suitors who had returned empty handed, tales of inexperience in relationships and drama that was reminiscent of one's high school years. No, Jzaleh was above all that.

Not only did I feel close to her as I felt we could talk about almost anything, but I was beginning to become emotion-

ally attached to her as well. On the days we were to meet, I could think of nothing else, and the days I did not see her somehow did not feel right. Still, a part of me was uncomfortable and hesitant. I felt our situations were completely different and that we were heading different ways.

I suppose we could have tried to stay the way we were, but the longer we did, the harder the breakup would be. I also knew this could not continue. Sooner or later, the pressure would build up, either from without or within, and she would ask me to meet her parents. What then? I was not a proper suitor, I did not have any means or even a job! The American passport certainly would help, but I was not even ready for such a commitment—we had only been seeing each other for a month or two.

Even if we were somehow able to maintain the status quo, I was not sure it was for me. The parties were growing to be as tiring as the ones in America. Furthermore, with the drugs and alcohol, they were just a means of escape, of forgetting and ignoring the present situation. And Jzaleh had become just such an escape for me. It would be hard, but I had to end it before we both would have become even more hurt.

We had met in Niavaran Park around lunch. It was a bright day, businessmen walking through the park, a few people having lunch on the grass. We sat on a bench. The tea sellers were carrying their wares calling out, "Cha-e! Cha-e!"

"Jzaleh," I said, "we have to talk."

She looked at me with mild surprise, lightly slapping my arm with the back of her hand saying, "You sound so serious—"

I couldn't wait any longer, so I blurted out, "I don't know how to say this properly, but I don't think we should see each other."

She now looked even more surprised before a look of concern swept over her face. She did not answer immediately but managed a weak, "Why?"

"Let me try to explain—"

She interrupted me, "Is there someone else?"

"Someone else? No."

Then she started to cry. This was the first time I had seen her cry. I wanted to hold her but knew it was too dangerous to do so in public. I tried to comfort her but it was useless. The one who delivers the blow can never be the comforter. "Jzaleh," I said, "I still like you a lot, it has nothing to do with you."

"Is it how we met? Does that bother you?"

"No, it's not how we met, but if it were another time, another place—"

Exasperated, she said, "I just don't understand you."

"You have a life here: family, friends, a future…"

"What future is that? You were the first good thing to happen to me in the last couple of years."

"Jzaleh, I have nothing here—no home, or family, no job."

"What about me?" she asked painfully, her teary eyes looking into mine.

"Don't you see, you are not the problem. It's me."

We were silent for a while, then she asked, "Then are you going to go back to America?"

"There's nothing there either. Sure I could go back and get a job, be a foreigner in a foreign land again, eat my chelo kabob *on the weekends, go to the parties, read my books, see a movie when it comes to town, and live in a world that does not exist. I am an Iranian and this is Iran."*

"No it's not."

"For now it is. Nothing has really changed in twenty years. The rusari's *hairline goes back and forth, but they are still here, they will still be here."*

"So you will stay in Iran?"

"Yes."

"But not with me?"

"No," I said resolutely.

"But you could rent an apartment, something…"

"My money will not last."

"But I can help you."

"That's only part of it."

"But you could get a job."

"I don't think I could take it, you know how it is here."

We sat in silence on the bench.

"Then what will you do? I don't like the sound of this... I'm scared for you," she said with a look of concern.

"I always thought I could live here, all those nights of going over my memories. I could not find a balance over there. I didn't like being the outsider there. I'm having a hard time finding a balance here, too, but somehow it's more manageable, I feel I can get it right. I don't know what will happen, but I want you to remember me this way."

I continued, "Sometimes I imagine the parallel life I would have led here if the Revolution would have turned out differently, if I had never left Iran. I think the two of us would have been OK now, don't you think?"

She pleaded while crying, "But I love you now, right here."

I could not answer her as emotions took over my powers of speech.

Mr. Soleymaani was sitting at his desk in his office, lost in thoughts that were as far away from the menial tasks that lay before him as he was from the world he was about to enter. Since he was between cases, all there was to do were the administrative tasks which he loathed. But he was the head of his department, and as much as he tried to be active in the field, there was still a lot of paperwork he had to attend to.

He was smoking a cigarette, and when he finished smoking it, he opened the next envelope from the stack on his desk. As he read this letter he became more and more surprised. It was strange, very strange. Mr. Soleymaani was strictly a guns and knives kind of person; murders were all he dealt with. But now he was being recruited for a political crime.

Mr. Soleymaani was the new man of the new times, one whom the system was proud of. He was self-taught. There had been no college or police academy. He had risen through the ranks of the *pasdars*, and when the situation quieted down, he settled into a job at the Tehran Police Department. Who better to hold a gun than him? After all, whom else could they trust in the burgeoning regime?

When he was growing up, violent crimes were unheard of, an occasional murder would make national headlines. As such, and especially after the upheaval of the Revolution, there was no real office, no systemic way of handling these cases. By the time Mr. Soleymaani found his way to the police force, the world was a different place, and he found a niche where there had been a void.

His experience as a *pasdar* had taught him how to be a policeman—how to hold and fire a gun, how to enter a dangerous situation. But it was crimesolving that attracted him. At first, he was guided by common sense. Then, he had studied the subject on his own—the theories, the practice. He had become the most prominent and successful detective in Tehran (and thus Iran), all but founding the Homicide Division. Therefore, it was not entirely surprising that he should be sought out to help in the case of a political crime. That is what the memo had said, anyway. What they really wanted was for him to head a task force to solve this riddle.

Mr. Soleymaani's immediate reaction was that he did not want to get involved in politics. He called for his secretary to bring him a cup of tea. He lit another cigarette and thought about it some more. He was through with all that. He did not want to be pulled out of the black and white world of homicide. But he knew this request had come from above, and to decline it was to invite God's wrath. He was no fool. He had benefited, indeed, was still benefiting from his close relationship with the ruling body. And now they were asking a favor. He was married, he had children. He had no choice.

He wrote a letter back stating that he would head the investigation but, as was his habit, his only request was that he work alone.

Day ?

I have been having the chills again. I feel I am at their mercy. And when the fever is not there, I am always anticipating their return. Only by writing can I keep my mind busy.

My descent from the Hotel Shams to the dormitory was relatively swift. I was now firmly rooted in South Tehran, where glimmer and affluence seemed like a distant reality. Through the years, projects were undertaken there out of necessity and not planning. The streets were noisy, tight, and cramped. The alleys were windy, taking unexpected turns when a building jutted out into or shied away from the street. Here and there, people had put up shacks with whatever material they could find. Within this chaotic maze was a uniformity of mood and tone. The variation between different streets was more in their names than anything else.

There were no trees to line the streets. The water of the joobs, *which had sprang from the pristine snow of the Alborz Mountains, had traveled southward, through all of Tehran, dragging down with it all of the city's misery and filth, delivering it to us. There were no trees for the* joobs *to water, and the water was not fit for any tree. But the people still had to use it.*

South Tehran has smells all its own. Or rather, the smells there are exaggerated, emanating from places they have long since saturated. This holds true for the pleasant aroma of the bakery and the musty odor of the tiny grocery store, to the repulsive stench of the blood-soaked sidewalk outside the butcher's shop and the fumes of stagnant urine rising from the lavatory in the mosque.

Those streets were stripped of any sexuality. The women all wore chadors, *either grasping it tightly under the chin, or biting it with their teeth if they needed the use of both hands. They darted swiftly to and fro, having fixed destinations.*

The only preoccupation was that of the daily bread. Only in the children could one see signs of life, but they grew up much too quickly, learning the art of hustling as readily as dribbling a football down the street. The men, if lucky, tended shop or had other work. Those who did not work would stand around all day, moving about slowly, sometimes gathering in larger groups, especially around the roundabouts.

The war veterans, the injured ones at least, were easily visible, arms or legs missing, relatively young, but usually with the proper prostheses as they received them from the government. Likewise, the Afghan refugees could be spotted easily, with their slightly darker skin, distinct accent, and unmistakably Mongoloid eyes. They reminded me of the Mexicans in California, powerless at the bottom of the social ladder, timid, easily taken advantage of, and abused. The refugees worked as cheap laborers, and also tried their hand at the black market.

The sick and destitute lay like wounded soldiers on the sidewalk, extending their tin cups or weathered palms for alms. Their deformities became their persona. Koor *Ali took the same spot on the sidewalk daily, his cane beside him, his small bowl in front of him. He was old with all his hair white. I never saw him without his stained white shirt and gray trousers which were fading at the knees, the white threads poking through as he sat cross-legged on the ground. He had a beard, and a round black cap rested on his short, greasy hair. Both eyes were scarred, the smoothness of his former eyes taken over by small clumps of protruding tissue which lay against a bluish white background, with a completely white center where each black pupil used to be.*

My path to the hotel took me by his spot every day. He would gently rock back and forth as he fingered his prayer beads, muttering a continuous stream of prayers under his breath, which was once in a while broken by the loud exclamation, "O God! Help this unfortunate one!"

As I went by I would say, "Salaam Ali Agha."

Sometimes I would drop a few coins into his bowl. I thought about him a lot. Was he just Koor *Ali with all his days spent in this manner? And what about Hossein* Shalleh? *He had to crawl on his hands everywhere as he was paralyzed below the waist.*

He would also take to a corner and beg all day. To be blind or lame and to have that erode every facet of your life until there was only one. Where the thing itself had become the beginning and ending.

One day I walked by and gave my normal salutation. As I passed in front of him I felt a blow against my right calf. I tripped and almost fell to the ground. After regaining my balance, I looked back. He was looking straight ahead as always, his cane in hand.

"I'm sorry Agha, I just wanted to talk to you for a minute," he said.

I crouched down beside him, resting my back against the wall.

"I hear you every day walking by here and sometimes you give me money, but we have never met. You must be new here, isn't that so?"

"Yes."

"What is your name?"

"My name is Arash."

"Where are you from? You have a bit of an accent, that's why I ask."

"I'm from Tehran," I replied.

He was quiet for a moment, his eyebrows squinting as if thinking hard. Then his face lit up and he said, "Yes, yes, now that I think of it, I know why I am so curious. You remind me of someone I met during the Revolution."

"How so?" I asked, now more curious than surprised.

"Everyone here calls me Koor *Ali. He called me Ali Agha just like you. He was young, like you also. He was one of those who had studied abroad. He would come around here talking* chert-o-pert*: equality, Communism, how we would all be better off after the Revolution. I am blind, I can't see a thing. But I can tell you nothing has changed."*

He continued, placing the index finger of his right hand

in the palm of his left hand while shaking his head, "The Shah did nothing for me." He repeated the same gesture, "Then the Revolution came and Khomeini did nothing for me."

He placed his index finger in his palm one more time saying, "That young man never came back. I have been sitting here for thirty years and the only ones who feed me and give me money are those who call me Koor *Ali."*

He paused and then asked, "But you, who…are you a Communist?"

"Me? No! I am a nobody," I said laughing.

He shook his head and said, "It doesn't make sense…"

"Would you like me to call you Koor *Ali?" I asked as I touched him on the shoulder.*

He nodded his head and took my hand and squeezed it. His hands felt coarse. "I prefer it that way. No need to call me Ali Agha here and then call me Koor *Ali behind my back. Anyway, there are so many Ali Aghas and* Hajj* *Alis here. It would be a lot less confusing."*

As I walked away my calf felt bruised and I was shocked at how a blind man could tell all those things by just hearing a few words from my mouth.

* * *

For a time I had a room in the bazaar.

I always thought the bazaar a distinct entity, a place that had no other function besides commerce. But this was far from the truth. At one time, the bazaar, or most of it, had been a regular neighborhood. As it expanded, it took over the surrounding area. The bazaar was situated such that the main thoroughfare, that maze that covered many city blocks, was where the storefronts were. Oftentimes, there was just a slab of metal siding going across the rooftops of the buildings, which at one time were across the same street. This made the bazaar an almost enclosed space, dark and

* *Hajj* – a title denoting deference, see footnote on page 11.

dusty with high ceilings. Rays of light would pierce through the cracks and holes above, expanding slightly as they came down, creating small spotlights on the aging stone and brick, and at noon they would come almost straight down, passing gently over those who walked through them.

The people were moving in all directions, some on foot, others with pushcarts or prodding their donkeys, and others riding bicycles or motorcycles, all in a space hardly the size of a car lane. Boxes, packages, rugs from all over Iran and the world were carried to and from the stores. It was this sound of motion, of all those objects brushing against each other, that was life itself.

There were tens, maybe hundreds of stores of each trade: carpet stores that hung their best Tabriz and Isfahan against the walls; stores with sacks of colored herbs and spices laid out in large bins with smells reminiscent of my mother's kitchen; textile stores displaying endless colors and patterns of cloth; jewelry stores with gold glittering behind the windows and a small scale on the counter.

The courtyards were usually off to the side, accessible through small passages and alleys. The backs of some of the stores opened to these courtyards, which in the old days were probably private residences. The room I rented was in one such place.

My window overlooked a small, run-down tiled courtyard which housed a few scraggly trees amidst the uneven ground that swayed up and down like the undulating sea. I could see the back window of an appliance store, empty boxes stacked against the neglected, almost opaque window. Below, there would be an occasional passerby and the smoky smell of kabob would drift up at noon. When I listened for it, I could hear the faraway rumble of the bazaar.

I always likened the courtyard to a small, serene oasis. Drinking my tea, sweetening my mouth with a lump of sugar placed between my cheek and back teeth, I would sit by the window and pass the time. Each sip washed over my mouth like a wave, clearing the sweetness with the slightly bitter tea. As the tea was swallowed, the sweet sugar would spread across my mouth again, marching forward like my thoughts. I would think about Jzaleh, wondering if I had done the right thing. Then there were the more pressing issues. I had trimmed my expenses but there was no money coming in.

I would sometimes stand outside one of the carpet stores. A green Isfahan with a beautiful medallion was hung on its wall. It was an unusual color for a carpet, green. I love the Iranian landscape, with its ashy brown terrain, its barren and rocky fields. Occasionally, this scenery is broken up by a stream with a Chenar *tree. But our landscape is altogether lacking in green, the color of* No Ruz sabzi *and the rice fields of the North.*

The owner of the shop did not pay any attention to me as he could see I was not a paying customer. After a few days, though, when he realized that I was unemployed, he came up to me and asked, "Are you looking for work?"

"What kind?" I replied.

"I need a helper. I have this small store, but I need someone to bring the rugs and spread them out for the customers. If you stay here long enough, I can give you that carpet at the price I bought it for."

I accepted the offer and began to work for Hajj Agha. *He was short and fat, sitting on his bench like Buddha for most of the day, counting the minutes away with his prayer beads. Once in a while he would get up and talk to the neighboring store owners.*

In truth, there was not much to do. If a customer came, Hajj Agha would suddenly spring to life as if a switch had been turned from meditation to action. I would have to haul the carpets out by myself and spread them on the floor, one after another, while Hajj Agha extolled the virtues of their pattern, color, material, knot, craftsmanship, and origin. When the customers left, I would have to fold them up again.

There was a small boy with a metal basket in our section of the bazaar who went around serving hot tea and collecting the empty tea cups. If Hajj Agha wanted tea when the boy was not around, he would say, "Arash, go and bring me a cup of tea." Also, at lunch I would fetch his chelo kabob. *If he was still hungry, I'd get him a second portion. He ate the same lunch every day and I could not help but think this was the cause of his rotund stomach.*

Sometimes he would teach me about carpets, the different knots and characteristic patterns of each region. The names of those cities were always enchanting for me: Tabriz, Isfahan, Kashan, Kerman. With the exception of Isfahan and parts of the Shomal, which I had seen as a child, I had never been anywhere else in Iran. I always had a longing to see those places I had only imagined.

One day he told me the story of the green carpet. "It is only there for show. It is a flashy piece to catch the eye of the customer. When they come in they usually settle for one of the more traditional ones. I've had it for ten years, no one wants to buy it."

All in all, I worked for him for several weeks. He never asked about my personal life. Hajj Agha wasn't nosy or maybe he thought it was beneath his dignity to associate with the help.

He had a deal with one of the tour guides who would come by with customers once a week or so. One day the guide brought an elderly German couple while I was away on an errand. When I came back, Hajj Agha had them already. A sweat had broken out over his brow as he had to lift and spread the carpets himself.

All that was left to be decided was which carpet they would walk away with. The couple had expressed interest in several including the green one. Hajj Agha pushed the green carpet with all the tact of a skilled salesman, using the right amount of persuasion and force when necessary. I was always surprised at how good he was at dealing with the foreigners. He went on and on about the special, natural vegetable dye that was used, the craftsmanship, stating that the rug was from the Shah's era, a real antique, in those days…etc. In the end, they took the green Isfahan over the others.

I was saddened but not much. What use had I for it? I never had a real intention of buying the rug, and I did not even have the money. Hajj Agha was looking out for himself, he had to, with the faltering economy and the sanctions. I understood all this but was disappointed anyway.

A few days later, Hajj Agha took me aside and said, "Let's go to the backroom, I want to tell you something."

I followed him there and Hajj Agha closed the door behind us.

"Listen, I've noticed that you don't ever pray," he said, "I don't want to interfere with your beliefs or religion but you have to understand. I pray every day. I have made pilgrimages to Mashhad and Mecca, I am planning to go to Najaf. Everybody calls me Hajj Agha. I can't have you work here like this. People notice these things, people say things, they would say, 'What kind of Hajj Agha is he?'

Now, if you don't want to pray, then during lunch, after I say my prayers here, come to this room and sit for ten minutes, I don't care what you do. You understand?"

I understood well and the next day I went up to Hajj Agha while he was sitting on the bench and fingering his prayer beads.

"Hajj Agha," I said, "this is my last day."

Hajj Agha looked up at me as he flicked one bead after another. He tilted his head ever so slightly and replied, "OK."

Hajj Agha did not bring it up the rest of the day, and when he finally closed the shop, he paid me and said goodbye with a smile and a taroaf *that were like all the days before.*

With the money I made there I was able to stay in the bazaar for a few more weeks. The dormitory was next. But I only stayed there a few days. Before I wasted my last bit of money there, I decided to spend money on food only. With the weather outside still good, hot during the day and mild at night, it seemed easy enough to sleep at the park. Anyway, I had become more sedentary over the months. At first, I had wanted to go everywhere and see everything in Tehran. I even went to Namaz Joemeh *once during that time. In addition, I had wanted to uncover all my childhood haunts, those places that had been buried in my dreams for years. But now I felt I had seen enough of Tehran and the park was good enough for me.*

They were right, in a way, my mother and the others who never came back. Memories do change. Mine are not as bright as before. If I had written these pages before I came, how different they would be! But the memories are still bright enough to keep me going. And for those that are lost or tainted, I have gained many more.

Now, I spent most of the day in Laleh Park, sitting on the benches by day, sleeping in the underbrush at night. Laleh Park had a seedy underside, overrun by drifters and addicts. I had to be constantly vigilant, and some nights it was difficult to sleep as there were so many arguments and fights, usually over drugs and money. Yet I had an affinity for that park that I could not easily part with: the weeping willows, the lush walkways, the tea sellers. I think they reminded me of the yard in the back of our old house. Just as the courtyard in the bazaar before it, the park had become my new sanctuary.

* * *

On those benches, I sat and pondered my fate in relation to that of our country. These were not new thoughts really, but with each step closer to the bottom I felt a clarity in my thoughts that was not there before. In over 2,500 years of history, of exalted history as we like to think, I could count all the just rulers that presided over us on one hand. Why did we allow this same pattern to repeat itself over and over, whether it be acceptance of the most corrupt leaders to the selling out to foreign interests?

We were to be the recipients of the great hope of the Revolution, but had become just another lost generation, lost abroad and lost here. After being beaten down, were we to roll over and die, or would we rise up again?

There was a truth to Behrooz's words that disturbed me. What could I, as one person, do that would have any effect? I wanted to be part of a movement. But there were problems. The Mojahedin *were the only ones outside the country with any sort of organization and clout, but they are just another thinly veiled dictatorship. Within the country, there was very limited activity. There were movements calling for reform, but all this was in context of the present theocracy. What was needed was a divorce of religion from government, which did not seem imminent unless done forcefully and violently. And that violent change could create a whole new set of problems, not unlike those since the Revolution.*

That the majority of the people were fed up with the Mullahs was a given. It was everywhere, from the cook I met in the bazaar who lamented the fact that "they" brought an Indian (Khomeini) to, in his words, "shit all over our country," to the truly devout Moslems who abhorred all the crimes done in the name of Islam. But it seemed as if everybody was caught up in the daily hardships of life, worrying where the next meal was coming from. Perhaps the collective memory recalls how we had sacrificed and lost it all once before and we are no longer willing to take such a risk.

If only we could take a calculated risk with the knowledge acquired from our past mistakes. Ghandi and civil disobedience appealed to me, but where were our leaders? I knew I was not cut out to be one; furthermore, I was without connections.

Within these constraints, my form of protest started to take shape. The idea itself came insidiously, I dare say subconsciously. The bastard's face was everywhere: on every billboard, office, newspaper. Nowhere were we free from him (thinking about it just now, thankfully, in prison I have yet to come across Big Brother's face), and nowhere was he more visible in daily life than the currency, the 500 and 1000 toman *bills.*

The 1,000 toman *bill, with beautiful shades of blue and green, has a mediocre drawing of Mt. Damavand on the back and Khomeini's stern face on the front. The first time, I only defaced his portrait. There was no great plan behind this, rather, it was just mindless doodling. As I was crossing out his eyes, a strange feeling came over me. I was conscious of the fact that I was doing something illegal. Spoken words are cheap, evaporating quickly as they escape the lips. What I had done was permanent, a miniature form of graffiti—Khomeini's eyes would never be the same.*

My initial joy turned into fear. What would I do with the bill now? The answer was fairly simple—put it under a clean bill and use it when shopping. And thus, the act of eating chelo-kabob *or buying groceries had become political.*

I continued doing this a few times. Then, I noticed that below his beard, on top of his right shoulder, there was a space where a few words could not only easily be written, but which escaped detection at first glance. I quickly progressed to statements, slogans, and questions:

Bogu Sheytan-e Bozorg Kiye? Haman Iman-e Ghola-biye.

Na Sharghi Na Gharbi: Na Jomhoorieh Islami

There were hundreds, maybe thousands that I penned in those months. Most weren't as long or clever as the ones I had seen during the Revolution but the ideas got across. I did not need a platform or newspaper, and these would reach those from all walks of life—that was the main point. There was a thrill as I penned them in the back of a taxi cab, or slipped the altered bills behind a wad of clean bills when paying for an item in a store. I tried to be smart about it, never having the evidence on my hands. I knew slighting Khomeini was a crime beyond all others, even worse than slighting the Prophet Mohammad or apostasy. Thus, I was extremely conservative at the beginning. I did not even tell Jzaleh, or Behrooz when I was drunk. I wanted all the bills in that city to be tainted, and for those who saw them to do some of their own. I had a vision of all the disgruntled people joining in this silent rebellion.

After a month or so, I began to grow paranoid. What if

there was a task force already targeting those who were seen writing on bills? Could they try to determine patterns of where the bills were coming from? To alleviate the fear of getting caught in the act of writing, I took to the practice of doing them in private. Also, in order to be efficient, I had to keep four or five handy so as not to miss an opportunity for dissemination. With these measures, I was open to other problems and, naturally, my paranoia grew without bounds.

Once I ran into one of my creations. How happy it made me feel! Even better, I saw one in circulation that another had written.

One day, I thought I saw Jzaleh walking through the park. I was sitting on a bench and only after she had walked by did I take notice. The faint trail of perfume was so familiar that it made me look up and see the walk that I knew well. How could it be? What was she doing in Laleh Park? But then I realized it was the middle of the day; she may have been to the bookstores. She walked for a while and sat a few benches away, opening a book. I wanted to talk to her but knew I could not. She would be repulsed. My clothes were dirty, I had not showered in weeks. But I did have enough courage to get up and walk closer to her bench to confirm that, indeed, it was her.

My heart was pounding as I neared her bench. Her eyes, those same eyes that had peered into mine, were glued to her book. She lifted her eyes from the book and started a quick scan up to my face. But she stopped before her eyes reached mine and resumed reading her book. I had become another nobody, another faceless inhabitant of this city. How I wanted her to see me, yet I knew this was for the best. I had nothing to offer her.

How sad I was after that episode! I could no longer bear to be in Laleh Park. I soon found a new dwelling in an abandoned building full of Afghan refugees. They seemed nice enough. That night they shared the food they had with me, bread along with a vegetable stew. A number of them were sick, lying in a corner or coughing, so weak that the others brought them food.

During the night one of them jumped on me while I was sleeping, searched my pockets, and ran off with my bag before I could do anything. Luckily, I had securely hidden my wallet and money on the inside of my pants, in an extra pocket I had crudely sewn on.

Shaken, I left the building and wandered through the empty streets of the Tehran night.

Mr. Soleymaani picked up the envelope and examined its contents. Inside, there were individual bank notes wrapped in small, clear plastic bags. All were 500 and 1,000 *toman* bills. A cursory glance did not reveal anything unusual. He then looked at the accompanying sheet and read the nature of the crime. He looked back at the bills, at the place the slogans were written, and smiled. Very clever, he thought. Mr. Soleymaani then looked at the sheet again. There were a total of 54 bills, roughly two thirds of which were the 1,000 and one third the 500 *toman* denominations. With this many in hand, he calculated that there could be 50 to 100 times as many in circulation.

Who would turn them in nowadays? He knew the majority of the people were against the government. Even if someone wanted to hand one in, they would think suspicion could fall on them. Had he been an ordinary citizen, he thought, he too would have done the same and passed it along.

That first day he came to several conclusions. Of the 54 bills, 51 had the same handwriting, the remaining three were each penned by a different author. If this was the work of one group as had been the previous theory, he would have expected the work to be divided equally, at least roughly. No, this was the work of one person and, statistically speaking, one man, as the overwhelming majority of political activists were men. Still, he wondered why he acted alone—it did not make any sense.

Mr. Soleymaani put up a map of Tehran with small flags signifying the locations where the bills were found. Most were in the central and southern sections. Did this reflect the base of support for the current regime and those who were more likely to hand in the bills, or did he live or work in those parts? This issue he left alone.

What was most baffling was the handwriting. Simply put, it was horrendous. The clarity of the phrases and messages was years ahead of the handwriting. Could he be almost illiterate, from a village, somehow never mastering the art of writing?

It was at this juncture that Mr. Soleymaani's progress halted. After that first day, he no longer had any new ideas and would stare at the bills for days on end. Every few days a new bill would turn up and he would dutifully put a new flag up. He knew he had to create some kind of profile or else he would never catch his man. But he needed more information, and this was hard to come by. One day while speaking to one of his colleagues, Mr. Soleymaani had said, "I must get into the mind of the killer."

"Killer?!" the man had replied, "I thought this was a political case."

"What are you saying? Oh yes, I can't get out of the habit of calling him a killer, you know how it is."

The killer was not one of them, he was one of the masses, and Mr. Soleymaani knew this was an obstacle to his investigation. Mr. Soleymaani had the kind of home that was considered anti-revolutionary during the Revolution, one of those belonging to the Shah, his cronies, or other landed aristocracy. As a friend of the Revolution, Mr. Soleymaani had been given the home, along with a chauffer and a bulletproof Mercedes with tinted windows. His home was a North Tehran mansion, with a swimming pool and a yard that was lush and vast enough to need two full-time gardeners.

Mr. Soleymaani knew that he had to give up these luxuries while on the case, at least while outside the house. He would have to live like an ordinary person in order to obtain more clues.

The first day after he came to this decision, he had his chauffer drop him off at the bus stop. Only when he arrived at the bus stop did Mr. Soleymaani realize his mistake. He felt self-conscious and silly as he got out of the car, with everybody staring at him, wondering what a person of his stature was doing at the bus stop. Then, there was the confusion when he boarded the bus as he did not know how to obtain a ticket or how much the fare cost. Even the driver had been rude to him, loudly saying, "Agha, which grave did you just crawl out from?"

The other passengers, who had already taken an interest in him while he was standing in line, burst out laughing.

The next day Mr. Soleymaani walked to the bus stop. This was a new sensation for him, not exactly new, but forgotten. He had told his chauffer to go on two weeks leave, paid. Not only had this made his driver very happy, but it also guaranteed that Mr. Soleymaani would have to take public transportation.

Mr. Soleymaani's house was located on a quiet street with only a few other houses. His neighborhood was full of old trees that climbed over the walls, spreading their shade to the street. He was far enough north that the pollution affected him less, and so he could still see, through the canopy of trees, the rising jagged rocks of Damavand.

It was a peaceful walk to the larger street. No cars passed him there. At the end of the block, he turned onto another street that was busier and a few minutes later he came to the first main thoroughfare. Here the cars were going by swiftly, two or three lanes each way, depending on the fluid situation of the moment. The fumes from the cars made him cough.

He had to cross the street. Mr. Soleymaani did so with the utmost caution, quickening his pace, awkwardly skipping, or suddenly stopping. Somehow he crossed the street. In the coming days, he would learn that the only way to cross the street was like a blind man, oblivious to the surroundings, whatever was to happen was God's will.

After crossing the street he walked over to the bus stop. His boarding went without a hitch, but he had not been aggressive enough in line and was one of the last to board the bus—he would have to stand for the entire trip. Although it was still morning, the sun had been up for several hours and the temperature was steadily rising. The movement of the air through the open windows helped cool him down somewhat, but he was still hot and the bus was crowded. The bodies of the men in front were pressed against each other, especially when the bus came to a stop or swayed from side to side.

It took him a few days to become adjusted to his new situation. He had to leave an hour earlier in the morning and came home an hour later at night. This meant that he had a lot less time to spend with his family at night, as he had to go to bed an hour earlier also.

On the third day, the bus broke down on the Vanak Expressway. The passengers got out of the bus and stood around, waiting to see if it could be fixed, but soon they realized they would have to find another way to get to work. Then a few started cursing the government.

"You know what it is...why can't we have better buses...or a decent metro? They say: Let's celebrate twenty years of the Islamic government, but they can't even get this right. They've had twenty years of government, they can't blame the Shah anymore!"

"*Gur-e pedar-e Akhounda*, may the corpse-washer take the lot of them!" one man said in disgust.

"What can be done?" another lamented.

"At least may God forgive and bless the Shah. See, this bus has been working all these years, since before the Revolution."

"You're telling the truth! Let me kiss your mouth."

Where did it all go wrong? Mr. Soleymaani thought. He followed the crowd in search of taxis and began thinking of his youth, and remembered quite well. He had moved to Tehran as a young man in search of work. In those days people did not address him as the important Mr. Soleymaani; he was simply known as Taghi.

Taghi did not want to toil in the fields like his forefathers. He envisioned them, his father and grandfather, as two in a continuous line of peasants. He saw his grandfather, aged and weary, still working until his death. He saw his father growing into the figure of an old man, still poor, still complaining about the lack of food and money. The land reforms that took place when he was a child had helped, that is what his parents had said, but the life he saw awaiting him was just not enough. He would not follow in their footsteps. He would leave the village.

Taghi went to Tehran in search of work but found something far more profound. Being without money, he gravitated to areas where he found others like himself. This was South Tehran, not that different then as now. He possessed only a few skills which were almost useless in a city. He came by work erratically, mostly odd jobs lasting a day or two. And once he had been hired to work in an orchard.

By then he had been in Tehran for months already. He had

seen the glitzy areas, he had walked along Pahlavi Street and no longer gawked like one who had freshly arrived from the village. The orchard had belonged to a person of affluence, there was no doubt about it. They drove to the estate in the pickup truck. It was off the road to Karaj, a lush and green oasis in the middle of the desert. There were high walls surrounding the estate and the green treetops were visible from a distance. They approached a gate manned by an attendant, who pulled the gate aside to let them in.

Inside, they saw all that the distant views had promised and more. The driveway was lined by trees, stout and blooming. A mansion soon appeared through these trees, dominating their view with its strange architecture and all-white facade. They got out of the truck and started to walk around to the back of the house. Lush green grass of a variety they had never seen before lay at their feet. Once in the back, they were greeted by an Olympic-size swimming pool. There was a fountain in the middle of it, forming a stream of water running down the hill, through a series of graduated slopes that disappeared out of view.

They followed the path to the orchard. They had been hired to pick the apricots that had come into season. They were to work in pairs and his partner was a young man named Hameed. When they had first entered the grounds, Hameed had turned to Taghi with a smile and said, "This is paradise itself." The orchard was vast and it would take the men, ten of them, all day to pick the fruit. None of it, their leader had told them, was even for sale. It was for the owners and their friends.

They spent the entire day picking apricots. Taghi even ate a few as he had no other lunch. They were so juicy and sweet that they sustained him all day. They were as good as any fruit found in his village, but much better than what was available in their part of the city.

At the end of the day, they gathered all the fruit and carried the crates to the front of the house. A few of the men had already finished and were standing in line to get a drink from the water hose.

The day's work was done and they began to talk about their plans for the night. The last few men, including Hameed and Taghi, were bringing the last crates from the fields. Just then, a white convertible drove up in the driveway and stopped short of the men. The young woman, who had been driving, got out and started walking towards them.

All the men stopped and stared at her. She looked like a model or an actress they had seen advertising soap on the billboards. She was wearing a sleeveless blouse and short skirt, and walked with a confidence that made Taghi nervous. Her sunglasses rested on top of her long, brown hair.

"You've just picked them?", she asked, without addressing any one of them in particular, "Let me try one of the apricots."

She started walking in Taghi's direction. He had become so excited by the sight of her that he had to pull up the crate to his midsection to cover his enthusiasm. But she stopped short of Taghi and picked up two apricots from Hameed's crate. Hameed smiled and said, "Please."

Taghi's eyes followed her every movement. He looked at her face and then her arms as she picked up the apricots, following the line to her underarm and turning the corner to catch a glimpse of her bra. As she turned her back to them and walked away while eating one of the apricots, the men looked at one another and began to grin. Hameed whispered to him, "Now you know why this is paradise."

Soon after, they rode back to Tehran. Taghi thought about her the entire way. She was stunning. He had never had a relationship with a woman. Furthermore, all the women he came across were different. The women in his neighborhood wore *chadors* and did not walk or talk like that. He could not stop thinking about her and the estate. Hameed saw that he was in thought and asked, "Hey, Taghi, what's with you?"

Taghi did not answer.

Hameed smiled and said, "I understand now…you're thinking of that girl. It's better that you forget about it."

Hameed's smile left as he continued, "I tell you this now Taghi: forget about her. Forget about her now. You will never be able to join that world."

Deep down, Taghi knew he was right.

From where he found himself in South Tehran, it was a stone's throw to the mosque. The sermons of social inequality gave eloquent meaning to all his life experiences. Moral degeneration, the infiltration of Western values that they spoke of, this he understood as well, but that did not stop him from thinking about her.

He soon began to get caught up in the foment of the Revolution. In the early days, when Khomeini was still in exile, they would gather around and listen to his tape-recorded speeches which had been smuggled from Paris. The bazaaris and the mullahs organized these clandestine events and financially supported Taghi, and others like him, for taking an active part.

He no longer had to work as a laborer. Instead, he spent all his time partaking in demonstrations, spray painting slogans on walls, or anything else that was required of him. Soon their numbers began to multiply and he was in charge of a small band, ensuring that every order from above was carried out.

By the time Khomeini finally arrived in Mehrabad airport, Taghi was part of the tight-knit group that would act as his bodyguards. And when the *komitehs* started to be set up all over the city, Mr. Soleymaani (no longer Taghi) quickly became the head of one.

He was there when they stormed the Shah's palace. Standing at the bottom of the steps, he knew this was a day he would never forget. He ran up the marble steps and through the large doors, in awe of the riches and splendors of the dynasty. He pocketed a small statue, payback, he thought, for the sweat of his fathers.

He was there when they started to confiscate other mansions. Most of the time the owners had already fled, but some had stayed behind. They were either thrown out on the street, arrested, or killed, depending on the temperament of the group of *pasdars* on that particular day.

He would see her again, that young woman in the apricot orchard—or someone like her—and this time he was in the position of power, in the position to do something about it. He had fantasized about her many times before, at night, by himself. But when the time finally came, the reality was quite disappointing. He had to be forceful and she cried the whole time. Moreover, although he was the first, he had to share her with the others.

He was there when they turned against the other political groups. He was there for the round-ups, the executions. Not many were sad to see members of the SAVAK or the Shah's inner circle shot. But the political killings that followed were harder to swallow.

It became hard even for him. One day they had brought in a young boy accused of being a Communist. Mr. Soleymaani had to approve the execution. In the past, he would look at the name or ask the *pasdars* for some information. The guilt was usually obvious. He would nod his head, and that would be the end of the matter. He felt no pity for the dying establishment, those who had broken the backs of his fathers. Likewise, hunting down the opposition, many of whom were armed, was easily justifiable. More and more, though, he was not sure who the enemy was and took longer and longer to approve the execution.

He questioned the boy in private. The boy was trembling. He said he was walking on the street when someone handed him a leaflet. He did not know what it was about and was beginning to read it when he was arrested. Mr. Soleymaani knew he was telling the truth. He looked far too young to be political. Even if the boy was lying, how could he be sure? There was pressure, though, for purging—from above, from below.

Mr. Soleymaani motioned for one of the guards to take him to a different room. He then told his subordinate to let him go, but to place a tag on him to get his contacts so they could arrest more people. The subordinate did not like that idea and they had a brief argument. In the end, he had to give into Mr. Soleymaani's order. Several minutes later Mr. Soleymaani heard a shot and ran into the courtyard. The boy had been killed. They claimed he was trying to escape.

It was then he felt the situation was slipping even from his own hands. He let promotions pass over him, and when the situation quieted down a bit, he requested a transfer to the police department. It was a move hardly becoming of a rising star, one who was there from the inception, but he took it.

That said, Mr. Soleymaani still enjoyed the perks of that close association. His position had made him an attractive suitor and before long he was married. In those days, all the things that were scarce or rationed could be found in his house. He had so much milk, meat, gasoline, and heating oil that he used to give them to his friends and family. Whatever was left over would be distributed among the people of his village. When he returned to his village, all of the villagers, even the elders, would gather around him and treat him like the *kadkhoda*. This reminded him of his youth, when he had left the village with dreams of coming back a success, bearing gifts for everyone. His dreams had come true.

He was now financially secure, and every day new opportunities sprung up. During his time in the *komiteh,* he even obtained a cut from the sale of the confiscated alcohol. Since he was the head, there was nothing for him to do but pocket the money. His hands were clean. Anyone else would have done the same. And in the police department, even now, for the right sum of money, he would place his stamp and signature on any piece of paper.

I drifted back uptown, living in the construction sites I had spotted earlier. Some seemed abandoned, with no workers showing up for days on end. I remember that during the war there was a set of twin high-rises that I could see from the window of my room. They seemed far away, on the horizon. The main frame had been put up, but because of the Revolution and the war with Iraq it had never been finished, a skeleton without inhabitants or furnishings. Looking through one of the tiny windows, you could see the sky on the other side. A crane stood nearby, gathering dust and rust like the buildings. Sometimes its long arm would gently sway back and forth like the hangman's noose. They stood for years like that. At night those buildings used to scare me—the idea of such enormous dwellings with no one in them.

I now lived in one. The ghosts no longer scared me, but I had to be wary of intruders. Luckily, in those relatively affluent parts there was much less competition and I never came upon others like myself. I did have to share the building with a gang of wild dogs, though. And at first this was not easy.

The notion that the touch of a dog was najess *was one of the changes brought by Islam. The ancient texts described how dogs were the most respected animal. To strike a dog or be neglectful in the care of a pup or a pregnant dog was a crime. Well, then came the Arabs…and we all know how that story ended…let us just say that time changes much, and dogs are now considered unclean. Some in Iran have dogs as pets, but they are considered the exception to the rule. So it was that no one spoke up for these master-less beasts, and silently or vocally encouraged their abuse.*

I know because I was an a active participant. In my youth we gathered in bicycle gangs to rid our streets of the enemy. Then as now, they were always a motley crew—mutts of different shapes and colors. They were all skinny, their ribs showing through their mangy hides. As no one fed them, I do not know what they ate. They usually napped under a tree by the joob *or other shady spots. They wandered through various neighborhoods in search of food and a hospitable place to live. Once they found a place, they would stay there until forced to evacuate, and then they moved on like gypsies.*

We hated them. They were najess, *bringers of disease. Back then, if you were to ask me if I liked animals, I would have shown you all my animal books and encyclopedias. I probably would have made an exception for a pet dog. But even I, who pride myself on never having been brainwashed by the regime at that age, had been hoodwinked by the mullahs. I take responsibility for those actions but the mullahs were at our side, our partners in crime.*

If one of us spotted the dogs, a few phone calls later we would gather into a group and search for stones. We placed these in the baskets in front of our bikes and quietly snuck up on the sleeping dogs. With screaming, hollering, and the throwing of stones, the assault would begin.

They would awaken startled and bruised, yelping as they ran away. They never fought back. They never actually caused any trouble. With our bikes we would chase them away, hurling our missiles all the while. Once we even cornered one and battered him thoroughly. Though we never stoned one to death I have no doubt we would have, given the opportunity.

And so the only dogs that ever approach you in Tehran are the rabid ones. Since those days I have felt a guilt about our escapades. And so if I even came upon a stray while I had some food in my hand, I would go towards the dog with a peace offering. But they always kept an enormous distance, cowering all the while, quickly ducking behind an alley or a parked car. The government had a concerted campaign of poisoning stray dogs, consequently, they were even more wary of people and handouts.

The dogs in the construction site were likewise reluctant to make my acquaintance. At first, they would growl a bit, but that was all. We stayed in opposite corners of the lot, each staring quietly at the other. We had several days of this peaceful, but strained, coexistence. Then, one day I took some meat and placed it at their spot while they were away. I did the same for several days and it was only a matter of time before their hunger got the better of them.

One night one of the dogs came over and began sniffing me. I gave him a bit of bread and petted him. Over the succeeding days they came one by one, or in groups, to greet me. I felt like an Achaemenid king presiding over court, being visited by satraps from all over the world. I named them all after historical figures. The ring leader, a German shepherd mix, I called Mohammad. His right hand man was also big boned, perhaps an Afghan Hound mix—he was the Caliph Ali. The gentle black mutt I named Cyrus, after the king. There were also two brown brothers who I dubbed as Khomeini's sons, Ahmad and Mostafa. The pregnant female was Layla. I was not sure who her lover, her Majnoon, was. Likely it was Mohammad, but the honor of the name went to the one with the best coat, a mix of black, brown, and white.

At night I would make a small fire and we would gather around it. I would take out my pen and a few bills. "Ahmad," I would say, "any tender words for your father?"

He was sleeping with both paws over his muzzle and did not even perk his ears.

"Ahmad, I implore you to please lay off the opium. I'm worried about you, sleeping all the time. We will have to talk about this matter later. What I gather from you now is that you don't fear him anymore, you are so confident that he will pay later that you can take the edge off with a bit of smoke, eh?"

I wrote on the bill:

Your time will come

I looked over at Mohammad and asked, "What have you to say for yourself?"

He looked at me and gave one loud bark.

"Let me get this straight. A fighter you always were, not always the kindhearted or forgiving kind like that Jesus fellow, but surely no worse than Moses. And you realize that you are partly

responsible for Khomeini in the first place…I mean, why didn't you clear up all this business with Ali and the succession before you died?…Do I hear a trace of regret in your voice?…Do you really want me to say that? OK, my good sir, I will not defy you."

Marg Bar Monafeghin: Kuse-o Khomeini-e Bidin.

"What do you think Ali?"

Ali was napping and gave no response.

"Ali, quiet on the issue, considering all sides, the morality of it all…"

I twirled the pen in my hand for a few moments, "Enough already, the verdict please:"

You are a blasphemer, oh Khomeini!

"And what about you King Cyrus, the founder of our most ignoble civilization, most fair of all kings, the true Shah-han-Shah, *the one who freed the Jews, the one whom Alexander admired—what have you to say?"*

I pet Cyrus as he lay at my feet. He licked my hand and looked up at me with affection.

"Listen up my fellow friends and colleagues, Cyrus wants to make peace. But how Cyrus? There is no religious freedom here. This is not your rule. The small reforms you are applauding can be taken back at any moment by the Velayat-e Faghih, *and how can one protest against a holy office? We are like medieval Europe with their inquisitions. There can be no peace with the Mullahs until religion is separated from the state. Then, the Mullahs can sit next to the Communists, Nationalists, and all the others. What do you say?"*

He licked my hand.

Democracy not Theocracy!

"Oh Laylah! Who do you hold in your belly? Please let it not be another Shah or Khomeini! Or another Baab or Mohammad, we've had enough madmen and bloodshed. Where are our *Ghandis? We turned our back on Mossadegh, the closest thing we had. And who holds the spotlight now? The* Mojahedin—*they would be worse than the Mullahs, worse than Pol-Pot. What about the*

Shah's son? Can we ever be sure he does not want to resurrect the monarchy? Tell me Layla, is there hope for the future?"

Layla's soft brown eyes looked into my own for a few seconds.

"Can what you say be true? Imam-e Zaman, *the hidden Imam is coming. He will come with the force of Rostam, you say? I would have preferred Ghandi but I suppose we have no choice, eh? Tell me if you change your mind."*

Imam-e Zaman *will make you pay, oh Khomeini!*

We spent our nights this way, gathered around the small fire, out of view from the street. It was then that I began to feel ill, feverish, with that God-forsaken cough. I kept thinking it would get better if I only rested. Some days I would stay in our hovel and the dogs would bring me scraps. Still, my health was deteriorating. Soon I was almost confined to that area, stricken with fever, chills down to the bone, pains in my chest, and a cough that was bloody. My memory from that time begins to blur.

One morning, while riding the bus to work, Mr. Soleymaani was staring out the window absentmindedly as the bus came to a stop. He was holding on to the pole that was vibrating with the turning of the engine, standing as usual, looking to see if any of the passengers were getting off so he could sit down. Two women entered his field of vision as they approached the bus. Both were young but one of them had an awkward walk. She looked Iranian but there was something odd about her. He looked at her as she boarded the bus and made her way to the back. She spoke fluently but with a slight accent, pausing unexpectedly, as if out of practice. She must be visiting from abroad, he thought.

Mr. Soleymaani's hand tightened around the pole as the bus started to move again. Suddenly a thought dawned on him. The killer was not illiterate. He was someone like her, that would explain the discrepancy between the handwriting and the ideas. He was someone out of practice with writing while still fluent in thought. Thus, he had to be young, 25 to 35 at most, and a recent immigrant. He now had something to work with. He had narrowed down the possibilities, from millions to thousands. There were still some questions. Was he acting alone? Did he live in the North or the South? How could he be found? Did Immigration keep good records?

That day he made several phone calls to secure the help of the proper authorities. It was a tedious task, making a list of the names of all those who had entered the country the previous year, then eliminating those who had left again. From this list he subtracted all the women, and all men over 35 and under 20. He was left with around 50 people.

He obtained the names and contact addresses of all of them and set to work. He personally tailed them, one by one, as they entered stores or went different places. None seemed to fit the profile nor were they disseminating the bills. There were a few on the list, though, who were not accounted for. They were the ones with addresses outside of Tehran. He went to Rasht and Shiraz. Eventually, each one checked out.

In the end, there was only one name left. His address was

in Isfahan, but when Mr. Soleymaani showed up there the family claimed they had not seen him in over 15 years. As Mr. Soleymaani walked away from that home, he knew he had the right person. This fit with the other clues of the case. He placed a surveillance team on the house and went back to Tehran in search of his man.

This was where the case would become exciting, when he knew he was close. It was no different than a criminal case, he thought. Methodical investigation and deductive reasoning, that was all that was needed. But he was now up against another obstacle. He had the man's name but he did not know where he was or what he looked like. They were supposed to send a photo from the Interests Section of Iran in the US, but it had not come yet.

Sometimes when I wake up in my cell, I must think for a few moments and rub my eyes before remembering where I am, and why I am here. But you can not imagine the astonishment and confusion I felt when I awoke with a blanket on me, lying on an unfamiliar bed in a room I did not recognize. I immediately thought it was Jzaleh's, but then I noticed a bed next to mine with an Afghan sitting cross-legged, quietly watching me. I looked at the door—it was slightly open. No, this was definitely not Jzaleh's. I got up and asked the man in the bed next to me, "Where are we?"

"This is a hospital," he said, in an unmistakable Afghani accent.

I looked around again. Was this really a hospital? It looked run-down for what my idea of a hospital was. The curtains were stained and the tiles on the floor were worn and faded. In the corner there was a sink with a leaky faucet and a dirty mirror. I had been clothed in a thin cotton shirt and pants. The Afghani man was thin as a rail and was coughing.

"What hospital are we in?" I asked after finally accepting the fact.

"Imam Khomeini Hospital. They bring you here if you don't have money to go to a regular hospital."

"How long have I been here?"

"Almost as long as me. I got here the day before you did, oh around a week ago. You were in bad shape. You kept yelling, 'Keep your money clean!' " He was chuckling.

"I thought you were crazy and belonged with the crazy patients, but they said it was TB and the fever making you crazy."

I did not reply, still being in shock.

"Yes," he said, "that's why you're in the TB room."

"TB?" I said dumbfounded, "How do you know I have TB?"

"Yes, they put all us with TB in one room, so the others don't catch it."

"Then what happened?"

"When you got here?"

"Yes."

"They tied your hands down with some rags, put a long tube up your nose to give you medicine."

I looked at my wrists. They were red and scratched. My nose felt strange now also.

He continued, "But you were so angry that they had to take the tube out each time they finished giving you the pills."

"It's strange, I don't remember any of it," I said.

"The doctors will be happy when they see you today, oh yes, you'll see."

And they came, one by one, and in groups. They introduced themselves as students, interns, residents—I didn't know the difference. One of them said that now that I was better he needed to do an examination and questioning. He seemed nervous and new to the job. After we introduced ourselves, the doctor sat down and started to ask many questions.

"Why did you come to the hospital?"

"I don't know. I woke up and I was here."

He flipped through the papers on his clipboard and said, "Yes, you were brought here. It says you had a fever. There is something here about a public disturbance."

When he mentioned a public disturbance, I had only the faintest recollection. I was lucky I had not been caught.

He was silent for a few awkward seconds, seeming to search for the next question.

"How were you feeling before?" he asked.

"Lousy. I had a fever and a cough."

"You had a cough?" he asked, looking up at me with interest.

"Yes."

Bolstered by a topic he could ask me about, he asked how long I had had it, if anything came up when I coughed, what color it was, and more. He went on to ask me where I lived. I told him Tehran and he did not get more specific. He asked if I had been out of Tehran. I told him I had moved from America less than a year ago. He looked up from his clipboard in disbelief before going over another round of questions.

While I was being interviewed and examined, a small congregation of doctors gathered at my neighbor's bed. There was one young doctor who seemed to be in charge. He directed questions at the others. He looked through some papers and sternly said, "Dr. Hedayati, how come there is nothing written in the chart from yesterday? Where were you?"

The one named Dr. Hedayati spoke up, "But we are not required to write every day."

"Since when?" the leader clamored.

"It's always been that way. Anyway, we had those lectures yesterday morning."

I could see the leader was becoming very angry. "Yes, for two hours you had lectures. Let's say you were busy until noon. What about after that? I know you all go home then, but you have to know all that is happening with your patients."

He looked through some more papers on the clipboard, flipping each page forcefully.

"This patient did not get his medicine yesterday."

He looked at my neighbor and asked him, "Did you get your medicine yesterday?"

"No, Aghaye *Doctor."*

He turned and asked the other doctors, "Why not?".

"He was supposed to buy his own," Dr. Hedayati retorted.

"But he didn't. You did not check up on him. I don't even know if you were here yesterday! It is your responsibility while he is here to make sure he gets the proper treatment. We could have given him one dose from our stockpile."

"He is not a baby that I have to hold his hand," Dr. Hedayati said with a look of disgust, "anyway, he doesn't pay for any of the services."

"I am sorry that you are setting such a bad example for the

interns and students. I am going to file a complaint against you with our chief. Now," he turned to the patient, "I am sorry about your medicine. I will get the nurse to get it right away. You should be ready to leave tomorrow, if our chief agrees."

"Thank you, Aghaye *Doctor."*

After all the doctors had left and we had the room to ourselves, my neighbor said, "Did you see that?! He is a good doctor. Most of the ones under him are lazy. I don't know anything about your doctors, but the chief of them all is coming tomorrow. Didn't you hear? I'll be leaving here tomorrow."

At night we talked to each other. He explained to me the workings of the hospital and the hierarchy, from the head doctor to the custodian. The Afghan's name was Abdullah. He was in his early twenties, single, and without family in Tehran. He had left them all behind in Afghanistan.

I asked him, "Why did you come to Iran?"

He started laughing, "Here?"

"What do you think? Look around you," Abdullah said, "we don't have anything like this in all of Afghanistan, even Kabul. The roads aren't like here, you can find anything you like in the stores here. Our economy is bad. Then there is the Taliban and all the laws we are forced to follow. People here complain about the government but they have no idea how good it is compared to Afghanistan. I had to leave. We were all so hungry. I left my village because the only work there was drug smuggling. I went to Kabul, but there was no work there either. So I came here to work and send money back home."

"And do you like it here?"

"It's better than Afghanistan."

"And how are you treated here, by the people?"

"We can work here and get paid and some of the people are good. Like at this hospital. I don't have much money, but they help me anyway. There are those who don't like us, they think Afghanis

are stupid and dirty, or that we are stealing their jobs. Sometimes they get angry and beat us up. What can we do?"

I remembered thinking that refugees are treated the same the world over.

* * *

The following day the head doctor came with an entourage of ten to fifteen people. They went to Abdullah's bed first. The head doctor asked a few questions, listened with his stethoscope, and told him he could leave that day.

Abdullah was overjoyed, thanking them all.

The head doctor then turned to me. He looked much older than all the other doctors. He had graying black hair, a trim beard, and was wearing a long white coat like the rest. He smiled and said, "Bah-bah...Look at you today. A few days of rest and medicine have done you well. How do you do? My name is Dr. Shams, I am in charge of this ward."

I shook his hand. He then asked the group, "Who will present his case? I want a full presentation with all the new information in the chart."

The one asking me the questions yesterday stepped forward and began, "I will Dr. Shams. The patient..."

I tried to follow what he was saying, but soon got lost in the abbreviations and terminology so I no longer listened. I turned my attention toward the group. There were both men and women in long white overcoats. The men wore shirts without ties, with the top button unfastened. Some were cleanly shaven, others with a bit of scruff or even a beard. Some had longer hair than the others. These were all clues to where they stood. The women had monteaus on, not a strand of hair showing. Still, I was able to pick out which ones would pull their rusaris back in the street, and would not mind a party at night. They wore the more stylish monteaus, and although they wore no obvious makeup, some had meticulously groomed their eyebrows and had applied some light creams and powder.

After the presentation, Dr. Shams asked, "Why is this case so unusual, can anyone tell me?"

They stood silent until one said, "He is not Afghani."

"That is true, but that's not the answer I'm looking for. Even though we see a lot of Afghanis here, anyone in Tehran can get TB *just by riding the bus."*

"Anyone?" he asked one more time. He scanned the group and his eyes rested on Dr. Hedayati. I now suspected that Dr. Shams knew about yesterday's episode. "Dr. Hedayati, standing in the back where I can't see him, what do you say?"

He thought for a moment and replied, "It has spread to his liver."

"At least tell me the name for it. Talk to me like a physician, not the corner grocer! Don't tell me it spread to the liver. In medicine we have a name for every condition. You are wrong anyway, try again."

Dr. Hedayati thought hard, his brows furrowed, shuffling his feet. But he could not come up with the answer.

Someone else said, "Miliary TB*."*

Dr. Shams continued, "That's right, Miliary TB*. Now, you just told me he came from America but was born in Iran. So did he get this in the last year or as a child? Regardless, we have to ask why does he have this now?"*

They all looked impressed, as was I. Those strange words were new to me, adding to my confidence in him. Once again no one had the answer.

"Come on, do any of you actually do any reading? Could he have something wrong with his immune system? Is he malnourished? He looks that way to me. What about AIDS*? Is he at risk for getting this disease? These are the questions you should be asking."*

When he said AIDS*, my heart dropped. He continued, "We do know that a certain number of patients get this, so maybe there is no explanation, or that we don't have a good one yet."*

When he said this I felt a little better. They continued their discussion about my treatment, delving into the intricacies, at which point I again became lost.

After the session ended, one of the doctors from the group stayed behind. He was clean-shaven and was wearing glasses. I knew where his sympathies lay and was not surprised when he asked, "What's America like?"

I told him about California. He asked me about the hospitals there, but I couldn't answer all his technical questions. They were much cleaner and better equipped, that I could tell him. He told me that he hoped to study there one day. While the doctor and I were talking, Abdullah was quietly gathering his belongings, all the while keenly listening to our conversation and looking in our direction.

By the time the doctor left, Abdullah was sitting on his bed again, with his bag next to him. He looked at me and said, "Look, we both came to the same hospital at the same time for the same illness. You came here from America, I came here from Afghanistan, and we ended up meeting each other here."

Abudullah then shook his head and continued, "Our meeting was ghessmat*."*

Abdullah was now smiling and I began to laugh. He picked up his bag and came over to me. We shook hands and said goodbye.

Over the next few days, the same doctor visited me even though I was not his patient. He told me about his family, about growing up in Tehran. When I continued to address him as "Dr.," he said, "Nonsense, call me…"

One day I asked him, "So what is going on in Tehran these days?"

He said, "Not much, one of my friends told me about a person who has been writing slogans on money. There are rumors of the regime cracking down on him, but I haven't heard it on the news or anywhere else."

This news came as a shock to me. "Did your friend say anything else?" I asked.

"No, you know how these things are. Rumors get started, everyone gets excited, pretty soon you think Imam-e Zaman *himself is coming. Then the thing is never heard from again. Maybe there is an arrest—sometimes even the authorities fall for it."*

I let the discussion end there.

Every day I would take the different colored pills. Once he brought my x-ray to show me. He pointed out the areas that were affected. But he told me not to worry, with the medicine I would be completely cured, but that I would have to take it for almost a year.

Abdullah was gone and I had the room to myself. Outside the window, I could see the patients being wheeled from one building to the next. There were some trees to look at also, and the sky beyond. It was actually quite peaceful and I enjoyed my days there. Most of the patients complained about the food and had their families bring them home-cooked meals, but I thought the food was quite tasty compared to the scraps I had been eating.

Sometimes I would go outside and take a stroll around the courtyard. I was alone for most of the day, but the staff was curious about me as they had heard I was from America. Thus, it was not unusual for me to have many visitors during the course of the day. Some of the conversations were funny, and I had to dispel quite a few myths.

The next person to occupy the bed next to me was an Afghan also. I was sleeping one night when I awoke to the sounds of commotion in the hallway. A stretcher accompanied by a few nurses entered my room and the lights were turned on. On it lay a ghost of a man. They gently lifted him up and put him on the bed. It looked like they were lifting a corpse. He was so weak that his muscles could not even support their own weight. One of the nurses connected a tube to a canister and then placed it in his nostrils.

"This is oxygen, it will make you feel better," she said, "I'll be back with the pills."

She left the room and came back a few minutes later.

"Now, can you swallow these or will I have to put a tube in your throat?"

I could not hear his reply but it must have been "yes" as she helped him up to a sitting position. She then gave him the pills. His hands were shaking and he dropped them onto his lap. The nurse picked them up.

"Now open your mouth."

He did so and she placed a pill in his mouth. She then brought a cup of water up to his lips and helped him drink it.

"OK, just a few more."

After he had swallowed all the medicine, the nurse then took the stretcher out of the room and turned off the lights. It was dark but I could see his silhouette against the light coming from the window. He was sitting up and I could not tell whether he was sleeping or not. He was breathing heavily, and with each exhaled breath he gave a little moan. I could not sleep for the longest time.

The next morning he was awake before I was. He was still sitting up and having difficulty breathing. He looked uncomfortable, and forced a smile when he saw me. We introduced ourselves briefly, somewhat awkwardly. When he spoke, it was always in short phrases, with pauses as he needed to catch his breath. His discomfort made me feel uneasy, so I kept quiet.

He was visited by many doctors during the course of the day, many of whom I had never seen before. But it was only later, when I was walking in the hall, that I found out how dire his situation really was. I overheard two doctors speaking amongst themselves. They said his situation was hopeless, it was only a matter of time, hours, perhaps days.

I went back to the room and looked at him. He saw me and nodded his head without smiling. He looked the same, breathing very fast. I knew he was badly off, but now I saw him in a different light. I could tell he was using all his energy just to breathe. He had no energy for anything else, even sleep. He was still sitting up, and every once in a while he would reposition himself. I felt sorry for him and wondered if he knew.

"Do you want anything?" I asked him.

He shook his head and said, "Thanks."

"Even a glass of water?"

He hesitated for a moment and I took this as a 'yes.' I went to the sink and got him a cup of water. I handed it to him and then sat on my bed.

"Thanks," he said, taking off his oxygen.

"I get tired of this…I feel human…when I take it off."

We sat there in silence for a few minutes but I could see that he was getting worse.

"Maybe you should put it back on," I sheepishly said.

"I'm tired," was all he said.

"It might help you."

With a look of defeat he put the tube back in his nose. I got up and went to the window. I tried to preoccupy myself with different thoughts, but all I could think about was that the man next to me was about to die. I had to get away. I spent the rest of the day in the yard outside. I even asked my doctors if I was well enough to leave. They said they would have to talk it over the next time they met with Dr. Shams.

I had to return at night. I had no choice. It was already dark and the lights were out. I heard his breathing as I entered the room. I quietly got into bed. After a few moments of silence, I was startled by his voice. All he had said was, "Salaam."

"Salaam."

There was a slight pause before he asked, "You're from America?

"Who told you?"

"One of the nurses…trying to cheer me up."

"Yeah, I lived there for a long time."

"Tell me about it…I always wanted to go…Especially now—"

"America is a big place. What do you want to know?"

"The hospitals…I never met anyone…from there."

I felt more comfortable now. I had seen enough hospitals on television to be able to put some things together. Even without that knowledge, all I had to do was improve on all I saw around me.

"OK. The first thing you should know is that they are enormous. Even bigger than here. And clean. They have people scrubbing the floors and hallways day and night. You can even eat off the floor and not get sick. The rooms are bright and clean, like a fancy hotel. The sinks have cold and hot water twenty four hours a day. Every room has a TV and radio, a bath and a shower. The hallways are white.

Now the doctors here are as good as any there, but over there, they have all the latest equipment, and all kinds of pills you can't find here. And there are experts in every disease."

"Do you think…they can cure me?"

"I have no doubt," I lied.

"What about money?"

"If you are poor then, like here, they don't charge you. It's all for free."

"You're telling the truth?"

"What do you think? Now where were—"

"How can I go…there?"

"God willing, when you get better, we'll figure out a way."

"But how?"

"I don't know, I suppose all you really need is a visa."

I paused for a moment and actually thought about his question. The thought of a destitute and dying Afghani who had come to Iran illegally, trying to get to America seemed ludicrous. He probably did not even have a passport.

"But now just concentrate on getting better…I tell you what,

you get better and I'll give you my passport, all you'd have to do is change the picture."

"You're joking?"

"Who's joking? I live here now, I don't need it. Also, if I ever want it, I would say I lost it and get a new one."

I was becoming uncomfortable and changed the subject.

"Now let's talk about something else…"

After that, he became quiet and did not ask any more questions. And so I went on talking for a while, describing what he would find in America: the people, the customs, the food, the climate. I, myself, was beginning to believe he would get better. After all, the doctors did not know everything. His breathing sounded less laborious and his moans were gone. I would give him my passport after all, I thought that night as I went to sleep.

I woke up at sunrise to the cawing of crows. I looked over to him. He was still in the same sitting position. The expression on his face was frozen. His mouth was wide open, his cheeks sunken in. His head was tilted back and his open eyes stared at a point high on the wall. I knew he was dead. I ran and got the nurse, who followed me back to the room. A few minutes later, one of the doctors came. He had been woken up by the nurse, still sleepy-eyed, with pillow lines across his face.

*He shook his head as he walked up to the bed, "*Bichareh*, he had no one. Can you imagine what it's like to die like this, alone, far from family and home?"*

"He wanted to go to America to get cured. I think he had hope until the end. I even thought that he was getting better last night."

He just shook his head and said, "He didn't need to go that far. Had he come earlier, then he would've had a good chance. It's a curable disease."

The doctor left and soon the orderlies came to take the body away.

Until then, my time in the hospital had actually been enjoyable.

But his death changed everything. Not that I would stay there much longer. As promised, they had spoken with Dr. Shams and he had given permission for me to leave. On the morning I was to leave, I was looking out the window when I saw a most curious sight. From the distance I saw two bearded guards, machine-guns in hand, running toward our building. At first, I thought it was out of the ordinary to be sure, but I had no reason to be suspicious. Then I remembered the doctor's words, that I had been the cause of a public disturbance.

I took a peek around the door and down the hall. I saw one of the nurses holding up several bills in front of a group of people. I knew I had been discovered. She must have come across them when getting my clothes.

There was no one else in the hall. I darted down the side stairs and out a side door. I ran through the busy compound. I tired at one point, forced to stop for a few moments to catch my breath before running out one of the driveways. I found some money in my pocket and waved it at the cabs going by. One stopped.

"Darbast, *Vanak roundabout," I told him.*

The driver nodded and I quickly got in. We sped away. I saw a few police cars coming our way. They passed by and when I looked back I saw them blocking off the hospital exit. In the cab, I had such a fit of coughing that my entire chest felt sore.

Once on the street, I was still wearing hospital clothes. I went into the first store I saw and bought a shirt and pants, taking care to dispose of the other clothes later that night in the fire.

I was anonymous once again. They had my wallet and knew my name, but they didn't know where to find me in this city of millions. I no longer even resembled the photo on my license.

That day Mr. Soleymaani received an unexpected phone call. He was told that a man had been admitted to Imam Khoemini Hospital with altered bills in his possession. Mr. Soleymaani rushed to the hospital but by the time he got there the man had already escaped. The entrances were sealed off and the entire property was searched, room-to-room, building-to-building. He was not found.

But Mr. Soleymaani now had the man's wallet in hand. He asked one of the doctors to read the names on the cards he found in the wallet. Mr. Soleymaani had been right, the patient had the same name as his suspect.

Mr. Soleymaani interviewed the staff and patients. There were two things he wanted to know: who this man was and how he got away. It was strange that he managed to escape. According to the nurse who made the discovery, she had called security immediately. They had come in minutes. And according to those who were there when security arrived, there was a big group of people standing around the nurses station, looking at the bills. He knew he must have exited from the side stairs next to his room. But had anyone helped him? The problem was that he had been there as a patient for a long time and almost everybody had had contact with him. Furthermore, no one had seen anything unusual that day.

The staff all told Mr. Soleymaani that the man was from America and each had a story or two about him. He was well mannered and did not complain, they said. One or two thought he was a drug addict, and a few took him for homeless. Mr. Soleymaani asked the doctors about the illness, the prognosis, and whether he had completed his treatment. The doctors told him he had only a weeks worth of treatment, and needed many more months.

When he was leaving one of the nurses said, "Don't worry, the kind of patients we have, they come back sooner or later."

As he walked away, he knew there were two things he had to do. The first was to have a team monitor the activity of each of the people who were there that morning, even though there was no telling if he could secure the necessary manpower and resources for the job. The other task, that of searching the streets, would be just as futile.

There were simply too many addicts and homeless. If this had been ten or fifteen years ago, the situation would have been different.

* * *

The next day Arash attempted to buy the medicine. He headed for Toop-Khooneh Roundabout. He had been there before, but only to make phone calls to Naazi from the main communication center. Now he considered calling her again, but what would he tell her? By the way Naazi, he thought, I have TB and am wanted by the government. Maybe he did not need to tell her all that, and he would call her just to talk to her, to hear her voice. But first, he needed the medicine.

At the southeastern corner there were throngs of men. They stood on the side of the sidewalk or in the grass. As Arash walked by, one by one, they whispered more than asked, "Drugs, do you want drugs."

Arash kept quiet and chose a spot where he could observe the transactions. There, men and women from all walks of life came in search of different pills, creams, syringes, and other supplies. After finding the right dealer they would go off together to a desolate place and make an exchange.

Mr. Soleymaani was there that day. He knew this was the only reliable place to buy medicine and that sooner or later Arash would show up. Mr. Soleymaani walked up and down the street, made a few inquiries about the drugs in question, and intently looked into every face he saw. Finally, he retreated into a corner like Arash. He periodically took out the driver's license and compared it to the passing faces.

Not far away, Arash finally made his move. Encouraged by what he had seen, he started asking around and was soon directed to the TB man. This particular dealer had all the pills for tuberculosis. He was young and from one of the provinces, unshaven and dressed in cheap clothes.

As Arash walked up to the dealer, Mr. Soleymaani looked at Arash. By then he had already examined hundreds of men. He concentrated on his walk, looking for any hint of foreign mannerisms. Mr. Soleymaani took out and lit a cigarette. There was nothing unusual.

He threw the match down and took in a deep puff. He now paid more attention to the face. As he exhaled the smoke, he looked at the license one more time and then up at Arash. Nothing registered. Mr. Soleymaani suddenly looked away at someone who walked in front of him.

Arash showed the dealer his paper.

The dealer asked, "When did you start taking this medicine?"

"Just a week or so ago."

"You know you'll have to take it for at least six months."

Arash had completely forgotten this fact. His friend had actually said a year, but he did not recall Dr. Shams saying anything about it.

"Is it expensive?"

The dealer nodded his head.

Arash showed him all the money he had.

"That will only get you a week's worth. Do you still want it?"

"Only a week?" Arash asked in disbelief.

"Yes."

Arash was disheartened and didn't know what to say.

"You'd be better off getting some opium or heroin," the dealer suggested, "do you want any?"

Arash shook his head and walked away.

The dealer called after him, "I could give you ten days' worth, but no more!"

Arash did not turn back.

The following day I tried to procure the medicine. I went to several pharmacies, but none of them had the medicine. They all had the same advice: I should buy from the black market. I went to Toop-Khoneh but the dealer said he could only give me a week's worth with the money I had. When I walked away he yelled that he could give me enough for ten days, but no more. As if three days would have made a difference. What could I do? Dejected, I hung around Toop-Khoneh all day with all the other lost souls.

I had wanted to call Naazi but no longer felt like it. At dusk, I walked south toward the bazaar to see if I could get some tea. I caught a glimpse of a man with a lighter in his hand, who seemed to be drawing on it.

I stopped and watched to see what he was doing. He was the same age as me and an addict. I could see it right away, from his clothes and demeanor, even before I saw the tracks on his arms. His eyes and hands worked in unison as he etched on the plastic of the Bic lighter. At the same time, he applied ink in the newly formed grooves, rubbing it afterwards with his thumb, which was stained black. There was an intensity in his face and a perfection in the curved lines that made me forget my own plight.

He had two or three done already. They all had the same scene. In the tradition of miniature paintings, the figures in the tiny frame were stacked on top of one another. In the distance, there was a small caravan of camels emerging from the desert and heading toward the walled city. Palm trees were visible over the city walls. The centerpiece of the city was a mosque with beautiful minarets and an ethereal dome. The turbaned prince, Majnoon, was the next character to be seen. Laylee, in the forefront, carried a faraway look on her face, tinged with a small measure of sadness. Perhaps she was unaware that her lover had returned from a long journey, or maybe the entire scene was her wish, her daydream.

The more I looked at the scene, the more amazed I became at how something so pure and beautiful could come from a place of such destitution.

"How much are they?" I asked.

He looked up at me and said, "Ye toman."

He continued working again. I asked him, "How about 600 tomans?"

"Dadash, look at this work," he said, stopping again and looking up at me.

"Am I not an artist? Is this not a work of art? What price can anyone put on it? All this work for each lighter, believe me, it takes a couple of hours to do each one—isn't it worth 1,000 tomans?"

I smiled for the first time that day, and I could not help but agree. I took out my small roll of 1,000 toman bills and was about to hand him one, when he said, "But if you give me some opium or heroin, I would take that as payment, too."

"I don't have any," I replied, again extending the bill.

"We could buy some opium, I would take a puff or two and you can have the rest. What do you say?"

I thought the hell with it, what was one week of medication, anyway, when I needed a year's worth? I had always wanted to try opium, and with all that had been going on, a small diversion seemed to be what was needed. I said, "Let's go, but you deal with the buying. The more we get, the more I'll give you."

He gathered up his lighters and tossed one to me. We headed for Seyed Ismail.

We waited at the street corner. There were others like us scattered about the street, some fidgety, all waiting for the same product from the same man. There was a beet seller across the way, and the aroma of cooked beets filled the air. I would have bought one but I didn't know how much money we needed for the opium. None of the others bought them either, their thoughts being dominated by a hunger for opium.

The beet seller was standing behind his cart, oblivious to the gathering of addicts. He had wavy black hair and a thick, bushy mustache that curled up at the ends. As the steam rose in front of his face, the distance between us grew further, making him seem *from another time altogether. The vendor lovingly tended his beets, turning them over periodically. Every once in a while, without looking up, he would shout,* "Laboo! Laboo!"

It was growing dark and soon the sad call to prayer was once again echoing in the streets. Finally, he arrived and we all converged upon him. When it was our turn, I observed their interaction. I did not sense any foul play. The dealer brought out a roll and I handed him the money. We walked back to my new friend's place.

"What's your name anyway?" I asked him.

"Jamsheed."

"You?"

"Arash."

"Do you smoke much opium?" he asked me.

"No."

"Well you're in for a treat. Nowadays the quality is very spotty, but this guy we got it from, he's reliable. There's no doubt about it—this opium is Reza Pahlavi *opium! Sometimes he'll even lace it with other drugs for extra flavor."*

He noticed I was coughing a lot and he looked over at me and asked, "What's wrong with you?"

"I have TB."

A smile broke out over his face and he slapped me on the back, "Don't worry a bit Dash-*Arashee, I had it myself before.* Bozorg mishi yadet mire! *A few puffs of this and you'll be alright, you'll see."*

He had a small, one-room apartment south of the bazaar. The room was filthy. Clothes, spoiling food, and papers littered the floor. We sat on the couch.

Jamsheed cleared the table with a swoop of his hand and brought out the vafur. *He spent a few minutes getting the charcoal lit and stoking the small fire. Finally, he placed the opium in the slot and quickly gave the pipe to me. He told me to first blow through the mouthpiece attached to the pipe. I did this and when he told me to suck, I inhaled the smoke and immediately began to cough. He started laughing and I passed it back to him. He took a few hits before giving it to me. I noticed he breathed deeper and held the smoke in longer than I.*

I tried the same and after several minutes a change came over me. My cough, I noticed, had subsided and the pains in my chest had melted away. Then a feeling of euphoria crept into my being. All the problems of the past and uncertainties about the future were gone. All that mattered was the blessed present, and every molecule of my body joined in that celebration. We both became quiet, stretching out on his couch. He said, "I was just going to tell you something, but I forgot."

I said, "Bozorg mishi yadet mire!"

We both started laughing.

"Bozorg! Bozorg!"

We smoked more and more and things started to get foggier and foggier. At one point he said to me, "Let me go and make some more tea."

Until then, I had not even noticed that there had been tea on the table. An eternity later, he actually got up to go. Alone, I took out the lighter from my pocket and looked at it again. The work was even more beautiful than I remembered. What I was looking at was no longer a representation of a scene. I was standing in the desert, outside of the walled city. I was in the shade of the palm that had reached over the wall. Laylee's and Majnoon's faces hung in the sky like the sun and moon. I trod through the sand, step by step, toward the caravan of camels, unadorned and without riders. The caravan came upon me and left, and Jamsheed never came back.

I found myself outside, in the night, walking in the streets of Tehran. I came to a joob *and tried to hop over it. But I landed short. My shoes got soaked and I scraped my shin on the concrete. I heard laughing, but looking around I didn't see anyone.*

Then I looked up in the sky. The faces of Laylee and Majnoon had been replaced by the Shah's and Khomeini's. I saw not just their faces but their upper bodies as well. The Shah was decked out in his military uniform, medals, stars, and stripes adorning his chest. Khomeini was dressed in his mullah garb, with the black turban of a seyed *and a black cloak draped over his shoulders. Their eyes were fixed upon me, and both were silent, looking serious. I closed my eyes for a moment. When I reopened them, they were gone and the moon was hiding behind the clouds.*

I continued to walk, my eyes avoiding the sky. But I still felt I was being watched. Looking at my feet, a light caught my eye. I looked up and saw a billboard advertising a movie. The letters were bobbing up and down, glowing and almost on fire.

I suddenly remembered something and looked up at the sky and asked, "Ahoy! Shah! Khomeini! Which one of you bastards was responsible for the Cinema Rex fire, anyway?"

They were there in the sky. They looked at each other before breaking out in raucous laughter. They could not stop laughing, as if it was a private joke between them.

I continued to walk and soon they were silent again. I looked up from time to time. By now their faces were continuously hovering over me, and they even seemed more expressive.

To say I had no idea where I was walking to would be a lie. When I got close to the destination, I looked up again and they both were winking at me. They were pointing with their raised eyebrows to the area by the street where the women were standing.

Most of the women were wearing chadors, *trying to capture the attention of each passerby with their movement and their eyes. I tried to gather my thoughts as I walked up to one of them. Just then Khomeini started to speak.*

"Not this one, the other one," he said.

I stopped in front of the woman and turned around. "What other one?" I asked Khomeini.

The woman gave a surprised, "What? Who are you talking to?"

Before I could turn around and answer her, the Shah said, "I'm coming right now to take care of her."

"Leave her alone," I said, "I'll do the talking."

She swung the handbag she was carrying, hitting me on the face, screaming, "Who are you taking to? Crazy man! Leave me alone!"

I ran away from her while pleading, "Shah, Khomeini, leave me alone!"

After calming down, I tried hard not to look at the sky. I walked further up the street and approached another prostitute. As I approached, she drew aside her black chador. *She wasn't wearing clothes underneath, and I saw her breasts that looked like two large pomegranates. My gaze drifted down her body but she closed the shutter. I had seen more than enough.*

"Salaam," I said.

She smiled and replied, "Salaam. How are you? Do you have the money?"

I showed her the wad of bills I was carrying.

She asked, "Do you have a place, or should we go to mine?"

"Let's go to your place," I said.

"It will cost a bit more, but that's fine."

"Let's go," I said.

As we walked away, I heard some chattering behind me. I turned my head. They were both nodding their heads in approval.

"Do not forget the seagheh,*" Khomeini said.*

"Not bad," the Shah said, "but you should have seen the beauties I screwed in my time: French, British, Arab, American, Iranian, princesses, beauty queens!"

"Don't think you were the only one who knew about the splendors of kingship," Khomeini said mysteriously with a grin.

"What are you looking at?" she asked.

We stopped walking. "Do you see the moon there, next to the clouds?"

She turned around and said, "Yes."

"Anything else?"

"No."

"Forget about it…"

"My name is Maryam, what's yours?"

"Arash."

It was a short walk to her place but all the while their voices were in my head: "Did you see her tits"; "Check out her ass, see how it pushes out of the chador*"; "I can't wait to fuck her."*

I was embarrassed and kept quiet.

She lived on a second floor apartment. She had one room to herself, but had to share the bathroom. After she opened the door, she did not turn on the lights. She slid off her chador, *took me by the hand, and led me to the bed.*

"Hey," the Shah asked, "what about the seagheh*?"*

"The seagheh?" I repeated.

Maryam laughed and said, "We don't need a temporary marriage for what we're about to do."

Khomeini said, "This is a sensible woman. Seagheh*—no* seagheh*—to hell with the* seagheh! *Just fulfill your duty as a Muslim man."*

I hugged Maryam and started to kiss her. There was confusion in the dark, and I felt so many sensations that I no longer knew what was going on. The Shah and Khomeini were yelling in my ears. After a while, I even felt the presence of their bodies in the room, on the bed. I didn't know who was grabbing what, and placing what where. I felt her breasts now and again as a point of reference, but there were also body parts I could not identify.

It was all very strange. Although uncomfortable, even repulsed by all that was happening, I went forth without hesitation as another part of me was excited and enticed like never before. We continued for a long while and I slept heavily afterwards.

I awoke in the morning when the sun shone on my face. I had such dysphoria, and initially only vague memories of the prior night. I felt utterly depressed after the high of the night before. I looked beside me and saw Maryam, and then it all came back.

She was lying on the bed, her black hair and youthful skin shining in the sun. She could not have been older than fifteen, I thought. Then I saw the blood on the sheets. Horrified, I grabbed her by the shoulders and frantically shook her.

Her eyes popped open and she pulled the blankets over her as she screamed, "What are you doing? Stop it!! Stop it!!"

I let go of her, "I thought you were dead—I saw the blood, I thought—."

"You are the one with cuts all over you. I didn't even notice last night. What happened to you?"

"I don't know."

"Do you have any drugs on you?" she asked.

I shook my head and fell silent. I started coughing as I put on my clothes. She lay there without saying a word. With each passing second my heart grew heavier. A fifteen year-old girl! Where was she heading? I had nudged her one more step in the wrong direction. A few more coughs reminded me that I might have even made her ill. Where was I heading? Everything I had done until then seemed to be all wrong and a feeling of worthlessness took over me. I started to cry.

She sat up in bed, concerned, and asked, "Why are you crying?"

I tried to talk but kept choking, "You…you…"

"What's wrong?" she asked again, walking over to me.

"I…raped you—"

"Don't say that, I did this willingly, for money."

I was shaking, tears streaming down my face. At that moment Maryam was the embodiment of Iran. As much as I wanted to, I could not explain this to her. All I could say was, "You are a runaway."

"So what? You would have run away, too, if you came from my family, with a father like mine." She went back to the bed and sat down.

I got up and put my hands in my pocket, drawing out the bills. A small bit of opium caught in the bills was now freed, dropping to the floor, tumbling to the foot of the bed. Her eyes followed it with the keen attention of a hunter. I handed her all my money and walked towards the door.

She called out to me, "Arash, don't leave like this. Gur-e pedar-e donya. *Come, let's smoke that bit of opium. At least we have that."*

I felt the lighter in my pocket. I turned around and went towards the bed.

* * *

I returned to our lot a man defeated. The dogs came up to me as before, but they too, seemed to be mourning. It was not until days later that I noticed Mostafa was gone. I was sick, and I had no money for medicine or even food.

How could I have done such a thing? It was not even the act itself but what it represented on a larger scale. I felt I was no better than the pasdar *who held a machine-gun to my neck, no better than the government official who takes a bribe, no better than anyone I had easily pointed my finger at. I have finally arrived, I thought, I have finally become Iranian. Yes, there was no difference between me and anybody else who actively or passively contributed to the ongoing misery of our country.*

Those depressing days passed by, one by one. Mostafa was by now surely dead, poisoned or round up and shot. I no longer left our hovel. I would lie there all day and once in a while the dogs would bring me a scrap. I had no intention of carrying out any more protests. It would have been hypocritical. I didn't have any money even had I wished to continue. I felt there was nothing to live for anymore, as I do now at times. As my illness slowly began to take hold of me, I actually welcomed it.

The only ray of light I saw in those days was the birth of Mehdi. One night, Layla gave a frightful howl and in the morning I saw three little pups by her side. It was a small litter to begin with, and in no time only one was still alive. He was a weak and sickly looking pup, but how he clung to life! Had there been even one more pup that was alive from the litter, little Mehdi would have perished. But now he had no competition for his mother's affection and milk. How touching it was to see the mother lick the baby's still shiny coat. And what a chore it was for him to feed at first, he would tire after just a minute of suckling.

Layla spent those first few days entirely at the hovel, so I had ample time to observe little Mehdi. There could have been no doubt as to what his name would be. The historical Mehdi, Imam-e Zaman, *it was rumored, was sickly and died as a child. But ours was to survive, I knew he would.*

I gave a lot of thought to Mehdi. What a beautiful notion it was, and how it appealed to me. This same prophecy has been told with only slight alterations throughout all the written history of Mankind. That there would be one born of lowly birth, who would come at a time when the suffering was at its most. And he would come, as if from nowhere, take on Goliath and set things right. Was there not some truth in that, had it not happened already? Did not Moses and Cyrus free the Jews? What about Jesus and his gospel of love? Even Firdowsi, the preserver of our ancient culture, was able to stem the tide in his own way. And we have a modern day example in Mossadegh, and Ghandi. Perhaps one such character is all a century, or even millennium, can handle. How I wished there would be one who rose, here, from these wastelands. How I wish I could find that person. At times I secretly wished that I could fulfill such a role, but a leader I never was, and I knew my heart was far from pure.

Little Mehdi slowly brought me out of the spiral of depression. Day by day he grew bigger and stronger. I spent hours playing with him. I taught him how to fetch a stick and answer to my call. He was the only one of the dogs that knew his name. At night he would sleep with his mom, but each and every morning he would call on me, waking me up by licking my face. He would be wagging his tail when I opened my eyes, eagerly awaiting what the day had to offer.

Even now, with my illness, at times I am able to get restful sleep. This sleep comes when I am most exhausted, usually after a paroxysm of fever, when my body regains the ability to regulate its own temperature. This sleep knows no dreams, save the last few scenes before awakening which I can only vaguely recollect. It is then that I feel like my old self again, healthy and fit, having never been acquainted with Evin or tuberculosis. My shoulders feel light and my chest at ease. New possibilities wed old feelings for those few moments before my eyes open.

And then they open with a flash of confusion and everything comes back into focus: it is a fall from grace as I see the wall in front of me, smell the stench of the cell, and feel my own greasy face and matted hair. Then it is time for that first cough that welcomes the day, usually the most foul and bloody, having pooled in my chest all night.

It is depressing to wake up this way, even worse than waking up from my nightmares in which I am actually happy to be in the cell. The nightmares are occurring more often. As a child, whenever I had a bad fever, I would experience the same recurring nightmare. When awake and thinking of it, even back then, it would not be frightful, but at night, in the midst of sleep, it was always terrifying. When I grew older the nightmares went away. Perhaps I no longer became as ill. But now, with my tuberculosis, the nightmares are back.

I am alone in the city. There is no sound, not even the sound of my feet on the asphalt. The other peculiarity is the heat that follows the light. The light is so intense and pervasive that it creates no shadows. The light carries the heat with it, a dry heat that allows no moisture, no sweat to form on the flesh. I wander through the streets and alleys in search of relief or a bit of shade. But none is to be found. I always find myself in front of the same building.

It stands alone on the city block, without a gate or surrounding wall. It has a long and austere façade; no entrance, no windows. There are gigantic tubular structures sprouting out from the middle portion of the building, flowing in both directions over its rooftop. Although the building itself is high, perhaps twenty stories, it has a squat appearance.

It is here that all the light and heat are coming from, and it is here that I am the most terrified, as if I am about to be tortured again. Paralyzed, without the hope of escape, I wake up with a miserable fever, unable to go back to sleep.

Last night I did not wake up at this juncture. I stood in front of the building and gradually my terror subsided, the heat receded, and a normal light returned. The building melted, forming a vast river that cut through Tehran. The streets were still deserted, the stores were closed and boarded up. A gust of wind blew a sheet of paper in my direction. I grabbed it and read:

Imam-e Zaman *thanks all Iranians exercising non-cooperation. Today, we shall gather by the river*

I saw that the entire city was littered with these papers, all with the same message, blowing through the empty streets. I walked beside the river and saw a dock in the distance. There was a single man at work, a carpenter, hammering away at what looked like small boats. I walked up to him, but he took no notice of me and continued to work, even after I greeted him.

Then I noticed a large procession headed our way. It was orderly but very noisy. There was singing and chanting. As it got closer, I saw that it was headed by someone seated on a powerful steed. I immediately recognized him as Imam-e Zaman. *Behind him were the Shah and Khomeini, walking with their heads bowed. Trailing closely behind them were bare-chested men, blood dripping down their backs, giving out cries of* "Ya *Ali!* Ya *Hossein!* Ya *Mehdi!" before each new self-flagellating blow with the heavy, metal chains. There were also the palm bearers, and others who carried large wooden floats that were draped in green and red. Behind them was an endless crowd of men, women, and children.*

The procession ended where I stood and everyone became quiet. Papers floated down from the sky, gently rocking back and forth as they made their way towards us:

By the power invested in me by Allah
I hereby sentence Mr. Khomeini and Mr. Pahlavi
to be fed to the boats
Imam-e Zaman

Imam Mehdi came down from his horse. He held a scroll in his hand. "This the list of those maimed, killed, exiled, and harmed by you two," he said.

He held on to the top of the scroll and pulled the tie. The rest of the scroll fell to his feet and rolled in the direction of the crowd. The people parted to let it through. The scroll continued beyond view, unfurling towards the horizon. Imam Mehdi then addressed the crowd and asked, "Is there any among you who says they are innocent? Speak up."

No one said a word.

Imam Mehdi then turned to the two men and asked, "Any last words?"

They both started speaking at once in their usual manner, Khomeini slow, cool, and calculated, the Shah with his air of self-importance. But none of their words were heard. When they saw this, they became more and more distressed, motioning and gesturing frantically. Imam-e Zaman *now spoke in a way I had not heard before, his voice reverberating, permeating the space surrounding us.*

"Your tongues are tied for those you have silenced. Lie in the boats!"

The two, as if by a power not their own, automatically walked over and lay in the two boats. They fit perfectly in them. Lying on their backs, only their heads stuck out of the boats, through a part that was carved out for such a purpose. A small, square-shaped wooden piece was attached there for their heads to rest on. The carpenter placed a wooden cover over each of the boats, hammering them with care. The lids had small holes drilled into it while the bottom part seemed intact.

"The coffin is for those who never had one."

The two coffin-boats were finished. Only their heads were now visible, the rest of their bodies being encapsulated by the wood.

"Bring the honey."

A swarm of bees approached and landed on the dock. They left a jar of honey, then flew to the other bank and beyond.

"Pour the honey."

The carpenter took the jug and poured the honey into their mouths. He slowly went from one to the other until their mouths were full. They swallowed some and gagged a bit, trying to spit it out, but it was useless—soon their faces were covered with honey.

"This is for your honey-coated lies."

A few flies landed on their faces, one by one getting stuck in the honey, specs of black against gold. Soon the urine and excrement would flow freely within the coffin, attracting flies that would enter through the holes in the lid. If they were lucky, they would die before they would start to rot alive. I saw all of this in that instant.

By the time they were ready to be cast away, their faces could not be seen anymore as they had become two swarming masses of black flies. Then I spoke up, "If we kill them, aren't we the same as them?"

Imam Mehdi looked at me tenderly and said, "I am not violent. Do not feel sorry for them, they are already dead, they were always dead. This is an example for the living."

He pointed to the crowd sitting in chairs in front of the river. The leading Mullahs were there in their turbans, the Royalists including the Shah's son, the Mojahedin, *the National Front, the Communists, and all the other groups were looking on.*

"Let them go."

The carpenter dragged the boats, one and then the other, into the water. They slowly made their way down the river. By now the banks were lined with people trying to get a glimpse of the two as they floated into oblivion.

* * *

I feel that it is now time to finish this story of mine. Day by day I am growing weaker while the fever gets stronger. Writing is becoming a chore.

When the fever reaches the brain it does terrible things. Reason abandons you. Inhibitions cease to exist. A new being is born that bears little resemblance to the one prior to the metamorphosis, a new being with a very short life span. It happened to me not once, but twice, and I fear it is well on its way again. I have become very adept at recognizing the warning signs. The illness magnifies until it has conquered all the body and then it reaches for the brain, the final conquest after which there is no other. The weakness grows, high fevers and massive headaches precede time unaccounted for and a growing confusion. The body gets so hot that it no longer feels the cold, even rain, or snow. And then it can become so cold that no measure of blankets or fire can bring relief.

I know that I am nearing trouble again because as I write this, flakes of snow drift between the bars above, landing on my hand, melting and evaporating quickly. I have ceased to feel the cold.

* * *

I found myself in Tehran. I was dressed in typical mullah fashion, with a black turban and tunic. A long time before that I had found the outfit in a plastic bag in a dumpster. I had a destination in mind and I thought it was best to go in disguise. God only knows where this twisted logic came from.

I could feel the eyes of all the people on me. School-age children gathered around me. They tugged at my robe and threw fruit at me. I didn't have the strength to fight them off. Taxis would drive by, refusing to pick me up.

Finally, I remember trying to call Jzaleh for help. Did I ever call her? Did she end up helping me? I can't answer these questions, but I have a feeling she did not. She would have been too concerned about my health to let me go. But I still imagine the following scenes:

We are together in her car, she picks me up at a street corner. I am feeling self-conscious and think she will be repulsed. She laughs instead, "You look even better than the first time I picked you up! How do you expect to get anywhere in Tehran dressed up as a mullah! This is not Qom!"

She has probably got over me, otherwise she would have been shocked, or maybe I just don't notice. We then go to my place and I change into my regular clothes. She says, "That will not do."

She leaves to buy some clothes for me. When she returns, I change my clothes and we drive to Khomeini's mausoleum. She drops me off on the road to Qom, right before the entrance. Was there a parting scene? Did she say something meaningful to me? Did I reply? Could I have said anything coherent?

I stood in front of the mausoleum. That I know for a fact. Perhaps, after that day in the park, I never saw Jzaleh again.

Even in my condition, I could tell this was a grand site. It had the basic architecture of a mosque, a golden dome as its centerpiece with four flanking minarets. I had heard there were grumblings from certain sectors of the Islamic elite, pointing out the fact that Khomeini's mosque had more minarets than Imam Reza's golden mosque in Mashhad.

By now it was night and the spotlights shining on the dome and minarets made them look beautiful. There was a huge line of people outside, and I thought this was the entrance. But when I got to the front I was given a plate of chelo kabob, *so I sat there eating the food with the rest. It had been a long day and I was exhausted.*

Most of the people there were the city poor and villagers, the women with black chadors, *the men with beards. After my meal, I walked past the peddlers selling socks at the entrance and went inside. I took off my shoes and handed them to the clerk in exchange for a receipt. I was searched before being allowed in the room with Khomeini. A sign read, "No cameras, cell phones, or blankets."*

I was so exhausted that I went into a corner of the large hall and slept. I woke up intermittently to cough or when there was a sudden emphasis in the otherwise monotonous sermon of the mullah.

When I woke up I was feeling much better. My head ached less and my fever was temporarily gone. I scratched my head and realized that the turban was no longer on it, and then I realized my clothes, too, had changed. I did not dwell on these facts too much at the time. But I remember all these things clearly, as if it happened yesterday.

I took a walk around the mausoleum. It was an enormous hall with very high ceilings. The vent ducts were exposed at the very top, but the sheer height of the ceiling and the colored lights and ribbons that hung from it did not make the place look too cheap. Perhaps it was still under construction. The hall was divided into sections, for men and women (brothers and sisters). It was pretty empty but for a few sleeping homeless and the occasional pilgrim wandering in. The lone mullah had gone home.

The main attraction seemed to be the free chelo kabob *outside, the lines as long as they were when I first came. There also was a souvenir stand nearby that no one seemed interested in. I went up to it and saw the photographs and postcards of the mausoleum. There were, however, no postcards of Khomeini himself. Curious, I asked the salesman if he had any. He replied, "No, but I have these."*

From behind the counter, he brought out a shoebox full of photos.

"These are all from the war," he said.

I looked through some of them. They were all photos of dead soldiers, usually on the battlefield. They had fought and died in the war we had fled from. Slumped over or dead eyes gazing skyward, flesh and blood was oozing from wherever they were shot: stomach, chest, limbs, and head. The war had long been over, but the dead soldiers did not seem a distant part of history. They were still remembered and grieved for by their families. I remember thinking, what if that cab driver saw a photo of his brother here?

Feeling disgusted, I went back inside the main hall. I had not expected to come upon such a thing there, but that event had nothing to do with what follows—my mind was set the moment I had put the turban on.

Khomeini's tomb was situated on the left side. The casket was in a clear glass room, with metal bars surrounding all four sides. The men and women were segregated, having to approach the tomb from different sides. The few pilgrims that were not busy eating dinner would go up the tomb and grasp the bars with their fingers, kissing the bars and the window behind. The glass window had long been grimy from the accumulation of the saliva and grease from all the pilgrims past.

There were two caskets inside, the larger one must have been Khomeini's. The other I assumed was his son's. Khomeini's coffin was covered with a large green velvet cloth and a smaller red drape on top. A Koran and a vase full of fresh flowers were placed on the coffin. High above the casket was a green chandelier.

Stepping back, I peered above. The top rim of the glass room was adorned with prayers from the Koran. The four corners of the roof, from the outside, had white vases and more flowers. There was a large distance between the top of this room and the dome of the hall above it. The dome itself, at least the part seen from the interior, was shaped like an octagon with intricate geometric carvings, a sort of abyss starting with large shapes on the periphery, decreasing in size to a point, which was the very center of the dome. An imposing chandelier loomed overhead, with tens of thousands of lights and attachments. The sight was dizzying.

I looked back at the tomb. There were slits in the glass where money could be dropped into the tomb. Most were small bills, 50 or 100 tomans. *They would fall to the ground in piles near the edges, although some were closer to the casket.*

I had heard of stories of people wrapping their feces in the money and dropping it in, stinking up the place. It had made me laugh when I first heard it; now I only smiled at the thought which also reminded me of Sir Buckley's parting request. I waited a while longer and went back to my corner. There was a bookshelf that was mostly empty. It had a couple of Korans and a few other religious books, none very appealing, so I took a nap. I awoke several hours later with a severe headache. It had come back along with the fever. I knew there was not much time left. It was only a matter of time before I ended up at Imam Khomeini Hospital again.

My head was throbbing and I felt nauseous, but I felt a sudden burst of energy when I realized that the time had come. I took a quick walk around. Everyone, including the one guard, was asleep. I walked up to the glass room. I took out a bill and wrote quickly. Then I took out Jamsheed's lighter and set the edge of the bill on fire. It curled as Khomeini's face started to burn. I carefully put the burning bill through the slot. Come on, come on, I thought, stay lit. To my dismay, the fire flickered out as it floated down.

I reached for another bill in my pocket but couldn't find any. I frantically checked all my pockets but they were empty. I quickly went over to the bookshelf and tore a page out of the first book I laid my hands on. One of the sleeping men stirred a little but did not wake up. I walked back toward the coffin. I put the lighter to the paper and slipped the paper through the slot. It floated down with the fire intact. The money nearby ignited. Soon the entire edge was on fire and the fiery bills rose with the flames. A few started to land on the coffin and the drape caught on fire. I had seen enough.

I walked toward the exit and quietly woke up one of the homeless men. I briskly made my exit. I heard cries of, "Fire! Fire!" behind me.

When I made it to the empty parking lot, I looked behind. There, I saw the light of the dancing flames reflecting off the wall. Smoke was rising from the dome. Barefoot, I headed for the desert in the direction of Tehran with a feeling of relief. I must have walked for hours and saw the break of day. I was by then confident that I had gotten away with the deed, but I feared what was to follow.

I am beginning to feel weary again, and there are several more things I want to write about, so I will leave them for later.

A few weeks after the first phone call, Mr. Soleymaani received another. The suspect had shown up at Imam Khomeini Hospital again. This time, there had been no escape.

That day another bill came across his desk. By that time, he had already heard the news of Khomeini's shrine being set on fire. The only serious damage was to the coffins: both had burned to ashes. The bill on his desk had been retrieved from the site.

Mr. Soleymaani examined the plastic bag with the bill in it. The bill was partially burned and he could not tell if it said '*Atash*' or 'Arash.'

He did not need a fingerprint analysis; he knew the handwriting by heart.

* * *

This time, when Arash awoke in the hospital bed, he was not confused. He knew exactly where he was. He had been expecting this. Nor was he surprised when he discovered his feet shackled to the bed.

But now, the entire mood of the hospital was different, as was his. The bed next to his was empty and the guards did not talk to him. The staff treated him differently as well. They kept their contact with him to a minimum.

The big event of the day was the visit by his doctors, but they, too, kept their distance and hastily wrapped up the loose ends of his treatment. He had even seen his friend once, and though he had treated him like he did not know him, Arash completely understood why. It was he who had run into Arash's room that day to give him money and warn him that the police were after him.

Thus, when Dr. Shams and his entourage came by he did not think too much of it. He thought they would only quickly discuss the relevant things in front of him and then move on.

Dr. Shams entered the room and said a dry hello to Arash, without his customary smile. He then walked up to the guard, with his young doctors in tow.

"Salaam, I am Dr. Shams, in charge of this ward," he said to the guard sitting in front of him, "with your permission I would like to conduct the medical examination in private. I will not ask you to unshackle him, only that you stand outside the door."

Dr. Shams smiled at the guard and said, "I think we have enough people to restrain him if need be."

The guard, a youth who was not yet twenty, looked too bewildered to answer and left the room without saying a word. Dr. Shams silently motioned for one of the students to close the door.

While everyone was engaged in the exchange between Dr. Shams and the guard, Arash caught his friend's eye and winked at him. He had smiled back.

After a brief presentation by one of the doctors, Dr. Shams addressed Arash.

"Now, after you left, how did you feel?"

"I was fine."

"For a few weeks?"

"Something like that, maybe longer."

"Did you take any medicine?"

"I went to buy some, but it was too expensive."

"And now you're back, under different circumstances."

Arash nodded his head and Dr. Shams began to examine him. After he was finished, Dr. Shams turned to the group and said, "This is an unusual and unfortunate case. I think a few of you were here during his last admission. Twice he has proven that his immune system cannot contain the tuberculosis. And twice he has proven that the tuberculosis is exquisitely sensitive to the medicines we give him. Only a fraction of people with tuberculosis will progress the way he has. He needs the medicine, it is that simple. Without it, he will die."

"While he is here, we can easily supply it, but out there," he said pointing out the window, "that is the problem."

Turning back to Arash he said, "Do you know where you are going after here?"

"No."

"I hope you have understood all that I said, and I apologize for being so blunt. But certainly now you must know how it is. It is not a disease that will relapse without a day or two of treatment. But it will come back, slowly, like a cancer, and it will surely kill you.

If you end up in prison, we will send a letter to that effect with you, but you have to make sure you get this medicine. If you end up on the street, likewise. Right now this is more important to you than food and water. Do you understand?"

"Yes."

* * *

After Mr. Soleymaani received news that Arash was better, he went to the hospital. Mr. Soleymaani walked into the room and took the guard aside. He showed the guard his badge and explained who he was, telling him to take a half-hour break. As the guard left, Mr. Soleymaani closed the door behind him. He then walked up to Arash's bed. Arash had his eyes on him the whole time.

"Salaam," Mr. Soleymaani said, extending his hand, "do you know who I am?"

Arash looked at him as they shook hands. He saw a middle-aged man, nicely dressed, sporting a beard. He did not know who he was, but he knew whom he represented.

"No," Arash replied.

"My name is Mr. Soleymaani, I have been the one tracking you for the past months."

"Congratulations, then," Arash said coolly.

"Well, I didn't exactly catch you. You made it easy, you came to us."

After this, there was an awkward silence.

"I have a job to do here," Mr. Soleymaani said, "the first part is done. I just need to fill in the details—for the trial."

"There's to be a trial?" Arash asked with surprise.

"Yes…I take it you acted alone?"

Arash was silent for a moment and then calmly asked, "What is the crime and what proof do you have? And don't I get a lawyer?"

Mr. Soleymaani sat on the chair at the foot of his bed. "Arash, the case of the money is open and shut. Your fingerprints are all over the ones found in Tehran; there was a stack of half-written ones in your possession. You even fled from the hospital last time. People have been convicted with far less."

Arash knew he was right. He also knew that even without solid evidence he would be placed in jail.

"You have no family here, right?"

"Yes."

"So Arash, you acted alone, right?"

Arash did not reply for a few seconds and then he nodded his head.

"That's good," Mr. Soleymaani said, his voice trailing off.

Mr. Soleymaani was silent for a few moments as Arash sank into thought. Mr. Soleymaani had an idea of what he wanted to say, but had no words ready.

He began, "Arash, I was a revolutionary, too, not that different from you. I think we all wanted the same thing. My father was a peasant, and so was his father, for generations. We were oppressed and lost in our own way. He changed all that, Khomeini lifted us all up."

"Was it you who he lifted up or your brothers?"

"Yes," Mr. Soleymaani said smiling, "he lifted me up. He was good to us like the Shah was good to you."

"And what good did any of it bring?" Arash flatly asked.

Mr. Soleymaani was becoming irritated. He ignored the question and walked over to the window and looked out into the courtyard at the people coming and going. Regaining his composure, he said, "Arash, you see, I know about the arson."

Mr. Soleymaani pulled out the small plastic bag from his pocket and walked over to Arash and handed it to him. Arash took out the bill from the bag.

"Do you know they already have two new caskets there, empty ones of course. No one in Tehran knows."

Arash looked at it incredulously.

"I've done my job," Mr. Soleymaani continued, "this is not even my field. They brought me over from homicide for this case…but I think I understand why you did it."

Arash looked up at Mr. Soleymaani, surprised by all that he was hearing. Mr. Soleymaani took the bill from Arash.

"Whatever you have done," Mr. Soleymaani stammered, "I have done far worse."

"I was rewarded," he continued as he brought out his lighter and lit the bill, "and you—you will be punished."

The bill was now burning and Arash looked at it as Khomeini's face started to burn. Mr. Soleymaani let it drop to the floor, and they both watched as it curled up, completely consumed in flames.

"It doesn't make any sense Arash, but let God be your final judge."

Arash stared at the smoke rising from the ashes and quietly said, "Whose God?"

Mr. Soleymaani did not have an answer. He had not even known what he was going to do or say before he came there. Maybe he had expected gratitude. But he knew Arash's fate, as did Arash, even without a second charge. As he turned to walk away, Mr. Soleymaani thought, I did what I could. If he does not appreciate it, it's not my fault—what can I do?

Still, somehow he was not quite satisfied when he left the room.

The death of an empire, like the death of an individual, is never peaceful. There are many ways to die and man has invented quite a number on his own. Like all sensations in this world, those related to dying are graded with factors such as the impending knowledge, accompanying pain, and the length of the process. I have heard some favor a swift death. Leaving aside the unpleasantness of the time preceding the actual event, death by guillotine would be one such candidate. But what of those few moments after the head is detached from the body—when the head rolls on the ground, feeling altogether new sensations and perhaps even seeing, however briefly, one's world turn upside down?

> *In an ideal scenario, we would all like to think that as we grow older and older, and weaker by the day, we slowly wither away, until one day we exit this world peacefully while sleeping, oblivious to all the turmoil within.*
>
> *Do not be fooled. I have seen it several times, in the sick and healthy. No, death is not a peaceful process. Once the elusive life force is extinguished, that invisible structure that keeps the organic machinery running, each part of the body is left alone, left to fend for itself in a losing battle. It is here that we are all joined in the end, no matter how we have arrived. As the villages and towns are cut off from circulation, their cries for help go unheeded by the other sectors. The king, himself, the seat of that most powerful function, becomes like all the others, fighting as one man for his survival.*
>
> *When Islam first took a hold of Iran, in the year 651 AD, Yazdgard III was such a man. History knows of his story, the last Sassanid king of Persia who met his end, alone, at the hands of a miller on the road to Merv. Khosrow was the miller's name and his motive was not political or religious. He had a baser need that ties all of it together: money. Khosrow, quite simply, murdered the king for the finery and wealth he still had in his possession.*

The story of Feerooz is only a footnote to the above and would be all but lost had it not been written down by his exiled grandson in China. Feerooz was the son of Yazdgard III, and only a child when his father was murdered and forced into exile. He, along with other Iranians, fled north and east, away from the invading Arabs. As he was the next in line for the throne, there was also a price on his head. Though they, too, were at the mercy of the locals, they would fare better than the murdered king.

From Transoxiana he wrote a letter to his sister, the wife of the emperor of China. The letter must have been similar to his father's. Because of the great distance, the Chinese had already rejected his father's plea for help. With the Arab army closing in on them, they could no longer wait for a reply that could take several weeks. Feerooz and his entourage embarked on a months-long journey, heading over the ice and snow of the Pamir mountains, and then through the desert wastelands of western China. Ravished, they finally came upon the Chinese outposts and made their way eastward to the Chinese capital. There, they sought refuge in the Iranian communities already established by businessmen years before.

Arash could no longer continue writing. His fever was back. He put his pen down and lay in the corner of the cell. He pulled his cloth over himself and tried to sleep through another bout of fever. Several hours later he woke up and started to think about Jzaleh. He wondered what she was doing at that exact moment. He tried to imagine a couple of scenarios, but this began to sadden him and he turned his thoughts to Naazi instead. Maybe she would become a mother soon. How happy his own mother would have been to have a grandchild. But he knew this would never happen and he became even more despondent. My mom, he thought, must have been where I am before she died.

A sudden wave of panic and fear came over Arash and he began to cry. He cried so hard that he began to cough, and he coughed so violently that his crying ceased. Soon, the coughing spell subsided as well. He looked at the notebook beside him and read the last few lines. I might as well finish this part, he thought.

When Feerooz was brought before the emperor, through the grand hall lined by soldiers, he must have thought of his own imperial residence half a continent and many dreams away. He walked up the hall, attendants following in procession, and made his way to the throne. What made a particular impression on the young boy were the emperor's golden boots and exotic robe. Feerooz, already emotional, knelt at the emperor's feet. The emperor picked up the boy and said, "You have come a long way. Have no more fears, for you are my brother and this is your new home."

> *Feerooz was granted 38 villages for his people and allowed to have a royal court in exile. For years, the Chinese emperor kept him close to himself, preventing him from going to the western battlefronts. But once the emperor died, Feerooz joined the ongoing battle with the Arab battalions that were pressing eastward. He won many battles but was never able to win back the home he was after.*
>
> *When he felt that death was imminent, he gathered around him his family, members of the Iranian community, and the Chinese nobility. He requested only a simple funeral. With all present, he looked westward toward Iran and said, "I have done what I could for my homeland, I have no regrets." He turned eastward and said, "I am grateful to China, my new homeland."*
>
> *Then he looked at his immediate family and the Iranians present. He knew he had lost the war, that it was all over.*
>
> *"Contribute your talents and devote yourselves to the emperor," he said to his children, "we are no longer Iranian, we are now Chinese." Then he died. Before he was buried, a horse adorned with a golden bridle and a gem-studded saddle galloped around his coffin 33 times, the exact number of victories he had achieved. He was buried facing west, towards Iran.*

Arash lay down once more. He thought about how this story, which had traveled over all those centuries, had touched him. He had first heard it a few years ago. It was this simple story that drove away any lingering reservations regarding returning to Iran. It was a story not different from his own, or others in exile. After some time, the Iranians in China were never heard from again and disappeared from the annals of history. This last fact had made a particular impression on him when he was in America—he could see it happening every day. He now turned to Feerooz's final words. Arash now thought that, unlike Feerooz, at least he did not have to look east nor west. Arash thought to himself, *Na Shargh, Na Gharb…*

As he looked up at the sky now, the same blue sky he had been looking at every day since he had been back, he knew he was home.

Glossary

Agha—Mr. or Sir

Aghaye—same as *Agha*

Ahre Baba—Yeah man

Akhound—a mullah

Akhoundi—of or relating to an *Akhound*

Allah Allah Allah, La Allah-ha-ill-Allah—Allah, Allah, Allah, there is no God but Allah.

Atash—fire

Bah-bah—my, my

Basiji—Islamic youth group or vigilantes that roam the city streets in search of offenders

Bichareh—unfortunate one, literally 'without remedy'

Bogu Sheytan-e Bozorg Kiye? Haman Imam-e Gholabiye—'Tell us who is the Great Satan? That imposter of an Iman.'

Bonyad-e Mostazafin—'Foundation for the Oppressed'—founded by Khomeini in 1979 with assets confiscated from those with ties to the Shah.

Bozorg—big

Bozorg mishi yadet mire—phrase meaning 'Don't worry, you'll grow up and forget about it.'

Chador—large piece of cloth used to cover the female body, leaving only the face exposed.

Cha-e—tea

Charshanbeh Suri—part of the Iranian/Zoroastrian celebration of *No Ruz*, the first day of the new year and spring. This event takes place on the Wednesday prior to the new year and is celebrated at night, when bonfires are lit in every street and people jump over them.

Chenar—plane tree

Chelo kabob—a meal served with rice and skewered meat (lamb, beef, chicken, or fish) that is grilled over a fire.

Chelo Kabobi—restaurant selling *chelo kabob*

Chert-o-pert—nonsense

Dadash—slang term of endearment meaning 'brother'

Dai Jan Napelon—novel written by Iraj Pizishkzad which was made into a popular TV series in the late 1970s.

Dakhmeh—'tower of silence,' referring to a complex, usually atop a hill, where the Zoroastrian funeral rites are performed, in which the body of the deceased is left to be devoured by vultures and other scavengers, as contact with earth, fire, and water is considered unholy. This custom ended among the Zoroastrians in Iran in the 1960s and is dying out in India as well.

Darbast—the practice of hiring a cab with no stops until the destination, rather than the customary and less expensive shared ride.

Dash—slang term of endearment meaning 'brother,' used as a title when addressing a person.

Fadaiyan-e Khalgh—'People's Sacrificers'—political organization of Islamic Marxists.

Ghessmat—'destiny,' usually used for only unforeseen favorable occurrences that imply the hand of God.

Ghorbon—'sacrifice'—as in: May I be sacrificed for you—a title of extreme respect.

Gur-e pedar-e Akhounda—a phrase approximately meaning 'to hell with / screw the Mullahs.'

Gur-e pedar-e donya—a phrase approximately meaning 'to hell with' or 'screw the world.'

Gur-e pedar-e Irani budan—phrase approximately meaning 'to hell with being Iranian.'

Hajj Agha—title of a Moslem who has made the pilgrimage (*Hajj*) to Mecca, often becoming their name, especially in the working and lower classes.

Hamshari—moderate newspaper published in Tehran.

Hejab—the name of any combination of garments used to cover the female body.

Hezbollahi—a member of *Hezbollah* ('party of God'), one in active agreement and support of the current regime.

Hoez—a shallow pool of water, usually rectangular, found in the courtyards of Iranian houses.

Imam-e Zaman—Mehdi, the 12th and final Imam of the Shia sect of Islam, who went into hiding (disappeared) as a child in the 7th Century AD, and who is to return on Judgement Day.

Joob—a trough of running water (sometimes seasonal) that, depending on the location, could be used as a source of water or as drainage of springtime run-off.

Kadkhoda—head of a village

Khan—Mr. or Sir

Khanoom—Mrs. or Lady

Khar tu khar—'donkey in donkey'—a phrase meaning confusion abounds.

Khoda beyamorzadesh—may God forgive (bless) her.

Komiteh—'committee'—local Islamic organizations that sprang up during the Revolution, and flourished after Khomeini's return to Iran, made up of vigilantes (*pasdars*) who imposed and protected Khomeini's Revolution.

Koor—blind

Korsi—a table covered by heavy blankets, with the area underneath heated by coal or electricity

Ku ku—a dish resembling quiche made with various vegetables such as eggplant or parsley.

Kuse-o Khomeini-e Bidin—phrase meaning 'the irreligious Rafsanjani and Khomeini'

Laboo—beet, beets

Mardeh hesabi—literally meaning 'honorable man' but often used sarcastically, giving the opposite meaning.

Marg Bar Monafeghin—phrase meaning: 'Death to the hypocrites'

Mojahedin—short for *Mojahedin-e Khalgh*—'The soldiers of the Holy War': National Council of Resistance-political organization of Islamic Marxists.

Monteau—a piece of clothing resembling an overcoat used to cover most of the female body below the neck.

Nah—mustiness (as a noun)

Najess—polluted, religiously unclean

Namaz Joemeh—Friday prayer for Moslems that, in Tehran, is held weekly at the University of Tehran.

Na Sharghi Na Gharbi: Jomhoorieh Islami—neither Eastern nor Western: the Islamic Republic!

Noonvai—a bakery where only bread is made

No Ruz—'new day'—the first day of spring, which is the first day of the Iranian new year.

No Ruz sabzi—in the celebration of the new year, *No Ruz*, it is customary to place a plate of growing wheat grass on a table.

Parvaneh—butterfly

Pasdar—the foot-soldiers of the *komiteh*

Pofak—an orange, cheesy, and salty snack resembling a cheese curl.

Polow khoresh—any number of dishes resembling a stew served with rice.

Reza Pahlavi—high quality item, like those theoretically found during the reign of Reza Pahlavi.

Rial—the basic monetary unit of Iran.

Rusari—veil used by women to cover their hair, leaving the face exposed.

Salaam Aleykum—May peace be with you; formal way of saying hello.

Salad olovieh—a mayonnaise-based salad resembling a cross between egg and chicken salads.

Sangak—a bread that is baked on heated pebbles in an oven.

Savab dareh—phrase meaning that the act or action under consideration is pious.

SAVAK—the Secret Service of the Shah

Seagheh—custom of temporary marriage in Islam which is contractual, lasting for a length of time (as short as one night) that both parties agree upon.

Seyed—a descendant of the Prophet Mohammad, male or female. The title is passed in a patriarchal fashion starting from the union of the Prophet's daughter, Fatima, with Imam Ali (the Prophet Mohammad had no male heirs).

Shaheed—a martyr

Shah-han-Shah—King of Kings

Shalleh—lame

Tak Tak—wafers covered with milk chocolate similar to Kit Kat.

Taroaf—a system of speaking using various hyperbolic phrases when in the company of strangers or, alternatively, as a gesture of respect.

Toman—the highest denomination of Iranian currency consisting of ten *rials*. At its best, prior to the Revolution seven to ten *tomans* equaled a dollar; in recent years it has been around 700–900 *tomans* for one dollar.

Tudeh—'The Masses'—a Communist political organization

Tu-sari—a blow to the head

Vafur—a pipe specifically for the use of opium

Velayat-e Faghih—'Guardianship of the Jurist'—a concept and political office created by Khomeini based on the following principles: all government until the second coming of *Imam-e Zaman*, Mehdi, is profane. Thus, until that time, the most learned and enlightened of the Shia clergy must lead the populace.

Ya—O!

Ye toman—'one *toman*,' slang for 1,000 *tomans*

About the Author

Naveed Noori is the *nom de plume* of the author.

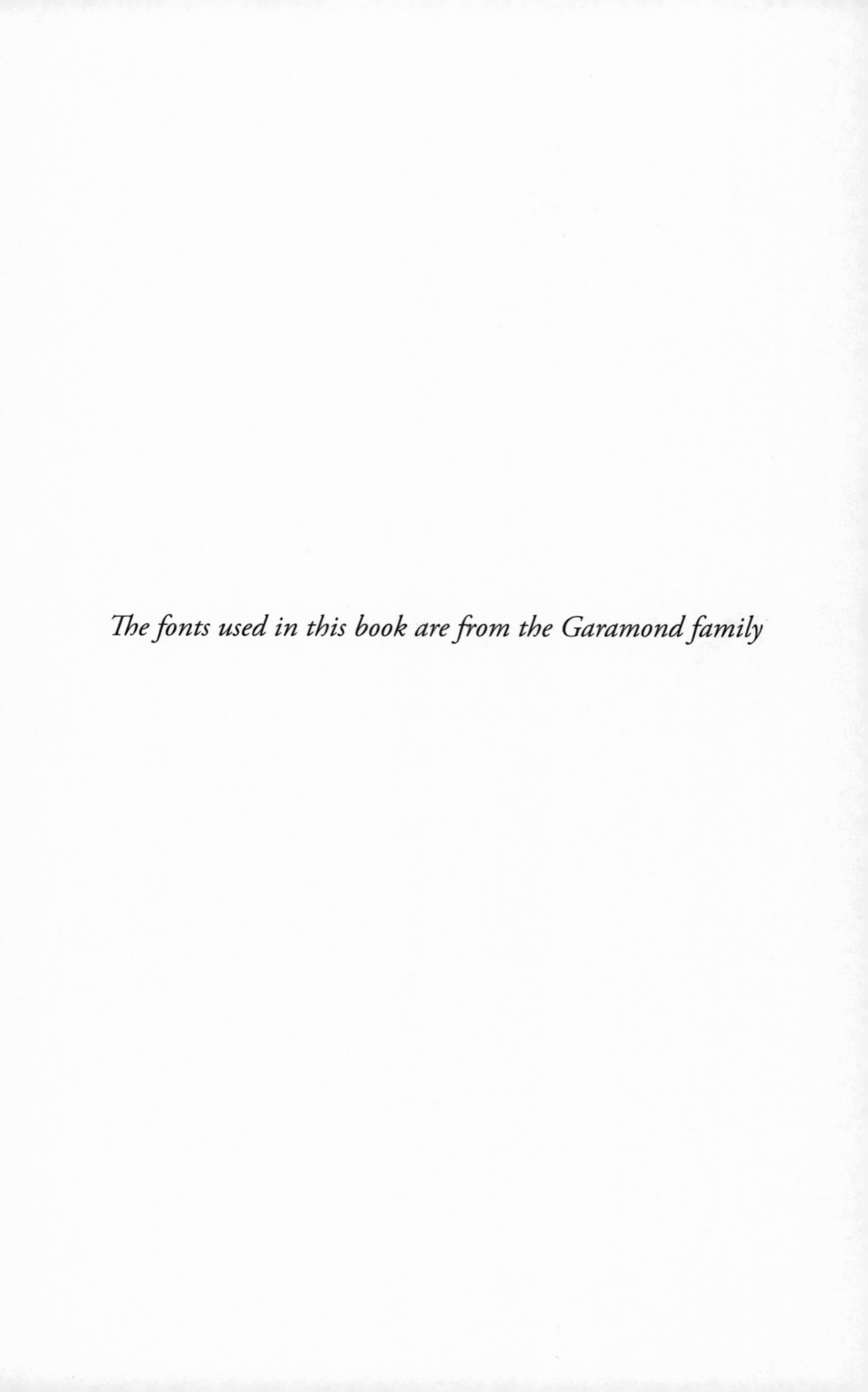

The fonts used in this book are from the Garamond family